Quickies – 10
A Black Lace erotic short-story collection

Look out for our themed Wicked Words and Black Lace short-story collections:

Already Published: *Sex in the Office, Sex on Holiday, Sex in Uniform, Sex in the Kitchen, Sex on the Move, Sex and Music, Sex and Shopping, Sex in Public, Sex with Strangers*

Published August 07: *Love on the Dark Side: A Collection of Paranormal Erotica from Black Lace* (short-stories and fantasies)

Quickies – 10

A Black Lace erotic short-story collection

BLACK LACE

Black Lace books contain sexual fantasies.
In real life, always practise safe sex.

This edition published in 2007 by
Black Lace
Thames Wharf Studios
Rainville Road
London W6 9HA

Typeset by SetSystems Limited, Saffron Walden, Essex

Printed and bound in Great Britain by CPI Bookmarque,
Croydon, CR0 4TD

ISBN 978 0 352 34156 3

Derailed Cal Jago

We had been waiting inside the tunnel for almost ten minutes. The carriage was heaving as usual – it was rush hour after all – and people were being their usual tetchy selves when it came to rail disruption. The air was full of tuts and sighs and commuters dramatically checked their watches or stood mute, frowning, with the odd 'can you believe it?' eye roll thrown in for good measure. The situation wasn't helped by the heat. A young man dressed casually in jeans and a T-shirt, who looked far too sleepy to be setting out for the day, pressed his right cheek against the door in an attempt to find some coolness. He had been standing like that, stooped and heavy lidded, for the past five stops.

I stood sideways on to the set of doors opposite Sleepy, my back against the glass separating me from the seated passengers, my briefcase held neatly in front of my knees. Just in front of me a woman with a rucksack bearing the slogan 'Designers are Crazy Bastards' was looking from the crumpled tube map in her hand to the map on the wall above the door and back again. To my right, a middle-aged man frowned into a book whose title claimed to be able to teach him Italian in seven days. I was sceptical.

The person who interested me most, however, was leaning against the doors to my left. Thick dark hair emphasised the blueness of his eyes and full lips pouted from a shadow of stubble. He held a rolled-up copy of Q magazine but clearly wasn't interested in it as he hadn't looked at it all the time he'd been on the train. Out of the corner of my eye I noticed him smile as the driver made a garbled announcement, indecipherable due to persistent crackling.

And then the lights went out.

Well, that really pissed them all off. As I listened to people complain and try to outdo each other by being more in a rush than everyone else – because their life was busier than anyone else's – I simply smiled and saw the situation for what it was: an opportunity.

The heat seemed to swell the moment we were plunged into darkness. An uneasy hush fell upon the carriage as the lights failed to immediately come back on as expected. I stood perfectly still for a few seconds as anticipation shot through my body like an electric force. My eyes gradually became accustomed to the lack of light and I began to make out the silhouettes of my fellow commuters. Bizarrely, Crazy Bastard still appeared to be hunched over her map, holding the paper up to her eyes in a desperate attempt to activate her see-in-the-dark super powers.

I cleared my throat and slowly reached down and placed my briefcase on the floor. As I straightened up, I turned my body so that I stood directly in front of Q. My skin tingled. In the eerily silent carriage the roar of my blood rushing in my ears was deafening. Then, ever so slowly, I took a small step backwards with my left foot and failed to suppress a sigh, which escaped from my lips and hung in the silent blackness, as my arse made contact with Q's thigh.

I shifted my weight from one foot to the other, the movement positioning my buttocks over his groin. I smiled. I knew he was smiling too; I could feel it on the back of my neck. I hovered there for a few seconds relishing the anticipation of the moment. Then, keeping the rest of my body absolutely still, I pushed my arse out slightly and finally made the contact with him that I craved. I remained still allowing him to feel the pressure of me against him. Then I gently swung my hips from side to side, exhilarated by the sensation of his excitement pushing against me. As I leant back into him more firmly every nerve ending in my body buzzed. This was going to be a good one, I could feel it.

Perfect timing then for the lights to flash back on and the train to lurch to life. Thrown off balance I reached up to grab the overhead handrail and in that split second the contact between his body and mine was lost. Feeling suddenly light headed, I gripped the handrail tighter as we approached the next station. I quickly looked around to see any obvious signs of my behaviour having been spotted. Crazy Bastard was now tracing a route along her map with her finger and Sleepy's eyes remained half shut. Elsewhere, the return of light had put reading and make-up application back on the agenda. No one appeared to have noticed mine and Q's small but significant indiscretion. As we roared to a stop at the next station, my tight chest and damp knickers and the presence of Q again nudging against my arse made it clear what I absolutely needed to do. As the doors whooshed open, I scooped up my briefcase, spun on my heels and flung myself on to the crowded platform.

I was swept along for a few frantic seconds, caught up in the wildebeest-esque herd of commuters until, at the mouth to the exit, the mass bottlenecked causing a jam. We stood packed together, all trying to pigeon-step our way forwards. Anxiety bubbled in my chest as I waited. I darted into a small gap and pushed my way up the steps, no doubt annoying everyone around me. But I had to get out. I had to breathe.

Once outside, I took a deep breath, filling my lungs with exhaust fumes and passing cigarette smoke and taking comfort in the roar of traffic. I looked at my watch and sighed as I began the long walk to the office.

My underground – and, for that matter, overground – train adventures could fill a book. Illicit liaisons with strangers in packed public places – what could be more delicious? There are times when the only thing that's got me through my working day is knowing that I'll soon be stepping into a new carriage, a new playground. Trains are my thing. I have lost count of the number of men and women I have teased, groped and generally been filthy with around the national rail network.

And yet, here I am having alighted four stops too soon about to walk the rest of the way to the office. So why have I just walked out on a great hit? Have I had a bad experience? Did I target the wrong person? Was I caught on camera and forcibly removed from a train and banned forever by Transport for London? No. Basically, I'm just trying to amend my ways. For the past three months I've been officially sort of 'seeing someone' and I figured that, early days or not, curbing my public-transport groping ways is probably the least I can do. But my God it's a struggle.

Dan and I met at a work thing. He had coveted the best art director award at a magazine do and so, when I found myself standing next him at the bar later, I offered him my congratulations. We already knew each other vaguely – same publishing house, different magazines – but our relationship up until that point had barely stretched beyond 'good mornings' and the odd eye roll in mundane meetings. But something must have happened that night as we celebrated with canapés and strawberry bellinis because a few days later, when he appeared in my office with offerings of a mocha and a muffin and asked me if I fancied going for dinner sometime, I said yes. I think he may have caught me off guard. Nevertheless, dinner the following evening had been a triumph and what followed that night back at my place, even more so.

A few months later all was going surprisingly well. And that made me slightly nervous. Not that Dan and I were serious. It was all just very light and fun and casual. And sexual. It's just that I'm very good at being single. I like to do my own thing, play by my rules and come whenever I like with whomever I like. And that's why I had almost gone into meltdown about Brighton.

'I've got to go to that conference next weekend,' he had told me through a mouthful of linguine one night.

I pulled a face. 'Lucky you. The agenda looks truly scintillating.'

'You're not going then?'

'Nope.' I had topped up our glasses with Shiraz and smiled. 'Budget cuts. They've almost halved the number of delegates and managing editors have been given the chop.' I took a gulp of wine. 'Damn shame. At least you'll be by the sea.'

'Come with me,' he'd said.

I had laughed. 'Are you asking me or telling me?'

He'd smiled. 'I'm asking you. But of course you have to say yes.'

I'd fallen suddenly serious. 'I'm not invited, remember?'

'I'm inviting you – as my guest in the hotel room. You can shop your way around the Lanes during the day, then we can do something in the evening. We could even make a weekend of it.'

I'd frowned. 'A weekend away?' I'd asked. 'Together?'

'Christ, Kate. I'm not asking you to marry me! I just want to take you to a hotel for a couple of days so we can quaff champagne and fuck each other senseless.'

Well, when he put it like that, nothing about the suggestion seemed to contravene any of my relationship-phobic sensibilities. So Brighton was on.

By the time I made it to my office I was almost an hour late and had already missed the start of a meeting. Natalie, my assistant, raised an eyebrow as I rushed in.

'Trains,' I said simply by way of explanation and headed for the meeting room. And despite my good intentions, flashbacks to Q and the possibilities of the journey home were already all I could think of.

The week passed quickly. Work was hectic and, besides meetings, I felt that I barely saw or spoke to anyone. At home on the Thursday evening I put on a CD and sank into my favourite chair, exhausted after another manic day during which I felt I had hardly achieved anything important due to the hours spent responding to constant emails. I was in the middle of convincing myself to never turn my computer on again when my front door buzzed and there was Dan.

'Brighton's tomorrow, isn't it?' I said rather abruptly.

He laughed. 'Yes. But it's not actually a crime to see each other on consecutive days.'

I wondered if perhaps it should be, but let him in all the same.

You know how you sometimes have evenings where you didn't set out to want to do anything or see anyone or make any effort at all and then before you know it something happens and you're having a good time? Or how you think to yourself, a quiet evening in, an early night, perhaps one glass of wine but that's it. And then you find yourself whooping and shrieking and laughing into the early hours convinced that you'll never come down for long enough to ever be able to sleep again? Well, that's how it came to be that Dan and I were both sitting on the floor of my lounge, smashed on an ancient bottle of tequila that Dan had found in my kitchen and sharing intimate thoughts and anecdotes with each other at four in the morning.

Through the highbrow medium of drinking games, I had learnt all sorts of personal details about Dan and had made a fair few revelations myself. The tequila, my tiredness, the intimacy and the varied sexual confessions had a potent effect on me; before I knew that I was even considering saying it, I heard myself boldly confess my most secret hobby.

'So I've touched all these men,' I was saying. 'And quite a few women. And I touch them until they lose all control and all they can think about is coming. People who would never think they were capable of such behaviour. But they do it for me, surrounded by all those people, because suddenly the only thing that matters to them is that I don't take my hand away.'

It was the first time I had ever confessed to it and once I started I couldn't stop. On and on I went, explaining how it felt, trying so hard to convey the absolute thrill of it. I was wet just talking about it. But it was a while before I realised that Dan had been silent for some minutes.

'What a dark horse you are,' he said when he finally spoke. He gave me a sideways look. 'Who'd have thought it, eh?'

'Have I shocked you?' I giggled and leant towards him to kiss him. I really wanted him then. I really wanted us to go to bed.

'A bit,' he said seriously as my mouth was just a fraction from his.

I hovered where I was for a moment before

moving to sit back down again. I frowned. 'I don't even know why I just told you that,' I said lightly. 'It's really not a big deal.' But the awkward silence between us told me it was too late.

Dan cleared his throat and slowly stood up. 'I'd better get going or I won't be in any fit state tomorrow.'

'You can stay if you like?' I said casually. 'It's late.'

He shook his head. 'No, I need to get home tonight.' He kissed me lightly on the top of my head. 'See you tomorrow.'

'Six o'clock at Victoria?'

He looked at me blankly for a moment.

'Brighton?'

He smiled and nodded and then he was gone.

Standing by the coffee cart at Victoria station the following evening could have been very *Brief Encounter* but, as it happened, it wasn't. Dan was nowhere to be seen. I tried to look nonchalant as I sipped my cappuccino and I attempted to shake the feeling that I must have looked like I'd been stood up. Or perhaps, the feeling that I really couldn't shake was that, actually, I probably had been stood up.

I hadn't heard from Dan since my revelation the previous evening and the more I thought about it, the more cross I was with myself for blabbing and the more clearly I recalled the serious expression on his face. Part of me believed that it was his problem if he wasn't able to deal with a small sexual peccadillo but I also felt embarrassed by my clumsy confession.

I still felt twitchy. Even if I was being paranoid

and Dan was on his way he was cutting it fine. There were five minutes to go before departure.

My phone beeped signalling a new text.

'Held up at work. You've got your ticket anyway so might as well just meet you at the hotel. Dan.'

I reread the message. It hardly sounded enthusiastic. Was this my cue to go home? Was its formal tone Dan's way of telling me not to bother? Or was I simply misinterpreting his message because I already felt on edge?

'For fuck's sake,' I muttered and then I tossed my empty coffee cup into the nearby litter bin and strode across the concourse towards my platform.

I glanced at my ticket; typically, my seat was in the farthest carriage. I hopped on board as lithely as one can when carrying a suitcase and wearing high heels. As the door was slammed shut behind me I stood wedged between it and the back of the man who had got on just before me. In front of him stood a queue of people, each shuffling forwards on a mission to find a seat. I gripped my ticket impatiently and sighed as I resigned myself to the fact that there was no point in trying to barge through to my seat. I would just have to wait.

On the opposite side of the vestibule area a man had already taken his chances, opting out of the shuffle simply to secure a decent standing space. He pressed himself back against the door behind him to allow the shufflers to move past him more easily. As the crowds began to disperse and I had progressed to standing in front of him, it struck me how perfect he looked. How absolutely my type. Approaching forty, he was dressed in a plain dark suit – Armani, I noticed, from the label inside the jacket, which was revealed when he removed it and slung it over one arm. His fairish hair was greying slightly and he had some fine lines around his pale-blue eyes. He looked a little quiet. Shy perhaps. Like I said: perfect. Even shy people need to let themselves go sometimes and when they do it's nice to be around to witness it.

As commuters began to move along the carriage I watched Armani gradually relax as more space opened up around him and I suddenly felt an overwhelming sense of longing. Apart from short instances of surreptitious train friction, I had been a very well-behaved girl over the past few months. No teasing, no grinding, no touching. And, oh, how I'd missed it. And now Dan was being an arse, my libido had gone into overdrive and here I was standing near the perfect Armani. Could I really be blamed if I were to seize this opportunity? Wouldn't it serve Dan right? And, more to the point, wouldn't it feel good to regain a sense of my old single self again?

Ahead of me a woman with four children and twice as many Hamleys bags was battling to get all her party along the aisle and safely into her reserved seats in the next carriage. She blocked the space entirely as she struggled. As I stood, lust momentarily gave way to irritation. I was irritated by the harassed mother for travelling with her brood during rush hour. I was irritated by her whiny children who continued to grizzle despite clearly having been bought half the contents of the world's most famous toy shop. I was irritated by my fellow commuters who did nothing to help her but simply exacerbated the crush by puffing their chests out and huffing loudly. I was irritated by the presence of Armani and the niggling thought that even though I wanted him I really shouldn't do anything about it although I tingled to my very core. But, of course, no prizes for guessing who I was most irritated with at that moment in time.

It was very appropriate, therefore, that on that thought the object of my fury came into view. The woman had managed to seat herself, the children grim and the numerous bags, so the crowd began to disperse. As I moved through the carriage and the crowd thinned as people found seats, my view cleared. And that is when I saw Dan sitting in his reserved seat reading a copy of *The Times*. I stopped suddenly and stared at him, amazed.

What the fuck was he playing at? He leaves me standing on my own looking like a social reject then annoys me with a grumpy text and all the time he was sitting on the train reading the paper? I frowned as I contemplated what to do. I was furious but I suppose it was petulant to make a point of standing all the way to Brighton on my own. And even if I did do that, what would things be like when we got there? Pissed off or not, I didn't want a weekend of awkward silences.

I sighed and started to move forwards but as I walked towards him a woman approached him and asked if the seat beside him was free. He looked up from his newspaper and smiled. Then, unbelievably, I noticed him glance fleetingly at me before telling her that it was indeed free as his travelling companion had missed the train. I stopped abruptly and stood still, incredulous. As the woman collapsed thankfully into the seat – *my* seat –Dan looked at me with a sly grin and an arched eyebrow before returning to his newspaper.

Shocked, I decided the best course of action was to retreat and gather my thoughts. Dan continued to stare at his newspaper but I could tell he wasn't reading anything on the page. I backed up until I was in the vestibule area again. Armani was now alone in the space. He looked up as I rejoined him.

'It's packed down there,' I said unnecessarily.

He smiled.

I snuck a peek at Dan as the door separating the vestibule from the carriage closed. Irritation had given way to curiosity now. I frowned slightly as I stared at him through the glass and tried to work out what he was up to. This was obviously a game. But quite what game we were playing I wasn't sure.

Armani had opened a book and begun to read. I was struck again by how attractive he was. There was something intense about him that I was drawn to; I liked the concentration on his face as he read. He was stockier than I had initially thought. He had a thick neck and strong forearms but I noticed that the hands which held his book steady were soft, his fingers on the book's spine, long and slim with perfectly smooth square fingernails.

A small train judder was required, I decided. A sudden lurch or a particularly bumpy stretch of track; all these factors that make a journey more uncomfortable for other passengers were things that I positively welcomed. After all, a girl has to reach out to steady herself if she feels herself falling. So I willed the train to jolt with all my might. And that's when a man with shoulders far too broad for public transport strolled through the door, forcing me closer to Armani in order to save myself from getting my ears knocked off. He lumbered through our space, pausing for a few moments to unwrap a sandwich. As he battled with the packaging, I made an effort to look terribly helpful and leant closer towards Armani to give Shoulders and his BLT more room to manoeuvre.

I smiled apologetically at Armani. 'Sorry,' I whispered as my chest made contact with his.

I was sure he blushed slightly as he smiled back. 'No problem.'

And then I slid my thigh between his legs.

Armani cleared his throat and shifted his weight slightly. I knew that the redness in his cheeks would have deepened but I didn't check to see. And I suspect that if I had looked at his face he would not have met my gaze. So instead I look at Shoulders who had accessed the sandwich but continued to look around in front of him, bemused.

'Here,' I said and reached across a little way and pressed the button to open the door.

He grinned and shook his head. 'Sorry. Thought it was automatic. Thanks.'

I increased the pressure of my thigh against Armani's crotch. Something was definitely stirring. 'You're welcome,' I said lightly.

As Shoulders disappeared through the door leaving Armani and I alone again, I did not move immediately. When I did finally, slowly, turn around, I saw Dan through the glass looking at me, his newspaper neatly folded in half on the table in front of him. He winked mischievously and, when I casually edged backwards so that my heels kissed Armani's toes, and his hardening cock grazed my arse, I knew that the game had begun. I just really hoped no one was planning on going to the buffet car any time soon.

I rocked against Armani firmly but slowly, resisting the temptation to grind like a harlot. My desperate desire to just grab him and fuck him there and then shocked me. But the reality was that playing in this sort of public situation you had to be as discreet as you could force yourself to be. Although the pair of us were alone for now, we were only separated from the crowds by a couple of sliding glass doors. The thought of that alone made me squirm in delight. But it was also a reminder that something a little more subtle than a full-on fuck in a vestibule was required.

I moved my hips slowly but rhythmically, keeping the pressure against him constant. His left hand moved to rest on the back of my thigh, the touch so hesitant, so gentle that it was barely perceptible. But I felt it like a flame burning through my skin. And feeling it confirmed that the games had commenced. The confirmation signal, whether it was a moan, a touch or a stonking great erection straining against my arse, was always a relief. Even if you are totally convinced that you've picked well – and that kind of complete conviction is rare – only when you've felt or heard or seen undisputable proof can you totally relax and really begin to enjoy the encounter.

His breathing became heavier as I increased the friction. As I moved, constantly aware of him pushing against my flesh, I imagined how he would look if I stepped away from him now and turned to face him. I pictured his face – flushed skin, muscles tight

– and, turning my attention lower, I imagined the impressive bulge in his trousers begging for release. Sometimes I abandoned them then, that image of utter desire and complete helplessness frozen in my memory as I left them in the carriage and lost myself in the crowd on the platform. But this time I was sure I wasn't going anywhere prematurely.

Armani's hand disappeared for a moment before reappearing on the back of my thigh, this time underneath my skirt. I held my breath as his hand rode a little higher, his touch still butterfly light. His fingers fluttered around the tops of my stockings. He skimmed the lace and pressed himself against my buttocks more forcefully. I did like a man who appreciated expensive hosiery. He felt harder all of a sudden as I felt his ridge pressing against the cleft of my arse.

I leant forwards a little, then reached back and ran the palm of my hand across the front of his trousers. A blast of hot breath prickled the back of my neck as I couldn't resist any longer and squeezed along his length. And that's when Dan stood up.

I continued to touch Armani as Dan edged out of his seat and began to move his way along the carriage, heading towards us. He gripped his newspaper tightly in his hand, the crossword page flapping open in front of him as he walked. He stared at me hard and I struggled not to squirm as Armani's fingers pressed more insistently into my flesh. Excitement caught in my chest as I wondered whether I had gone too far. Dan's expression was unreadable as he came closer but he walked with purpose, his gaze never leaving mine. I probably should have played it safe and stopped doing what

I was doing. Stroking a stranger's cock when the man you're sort of seeing is approaching is probably, on the whole, unwise. But I couldn't stop myself. I couldn't let him go. I had waited months for this and the knowledge that Dan knew what I was doing and knew that he had been watching turned me on even more.

Dan hesitated just as he arrived at the other side of the door and that's when he let his newspaper fall to his side and I saw that I didn't need to worry about having gone too far. It was very clear that he had enjoyed the show. Only then did I realise that Armani obviously had no idea that Dan was there and that we could be seen. I assumed that Armani had his eyes shut. Obviously, he was not used to playing in public. Closing one's eyes in such a situation was potentially dangerous, as he was about to find out.

As the door whooshed open, Armani's body froze in an instant – apart from his hand which rocketed out from under my skirt and then rested limply at his side. Dan moved into our space and then stopped. My right hand still held Armani's cock but I had become still too. Dan did not look at either of us at all, but straightened his newspaper up and then folded it and turned it over so that he was looking at the top half of the back page. Sport. Not Dan's thing at all but then I didn't believe for one second that he was reading it. I realised that, standing behind me, Armani would not have been able to see Dan's obvious arousal. As far as he was concerned, this was a stranger who had walked in on our indiscretion – whether he had seen everything or not he wasn't sure – so probably the best thing to do in his mind was to shrink into the background. I had other plans though. I couldn't let Armani be too mortified or scared. More to the point, I couldn't have that cock of his go to waste.

So I slowly reached back and touched him again, my gaze never once leaving Dan who I am sure, out of the corner of his eye, could see that play had resumed. I couldn't help but breathe a small sigh of relief when I gripped Armani again and found he was still hard. His entire body was tense, however, so the possibility of him losing his nerve and taking flight was still very real. We had to play this absolutely right or we would lose him.

I continued to squeeze along his length, gently but firmly. I kept my body movement minimal so that Armani could see that I was still being discreet but still his body felt tense behind me. Gripping him firmly, I began to rub him through his trousers, strokes as long and smooth as I could get them through the material and from the difficult angle I was working from. Then I worked my hand lower and reached back between his legs. He felt heavy in my hand, his balls cupped in my palm. I squeezed them before returning to stroke his shaft again. Bingo. Despite his severe reservations he was relaxing. His body wanted this as much as mine did.

I noticed Dan quickly glance around checking that no one was coming through either door. He took a couple of steps closer towards us and then, as he looked down at the sports page again, he pushed his right hand up the front of my skirt and slid his fingers over my underwear. Taken by surprise, I barely stifled a moan. I bit down on my bottom lip, painfully aware of how wet the material was on his fingertips. I continued to watch his face as he continued to stare at the newspaper. He was good; an expression of pure concentration, apparently focused on the sports report, remained on his face while his fingers roamed over my underwear, lingering maddeningly but never staying in one place for quite long enough. Divine frustration. I wondered whether Armani's eyes were open now and, if so, whether he could see where Dan's hand was. Did he know that he was part of our game? Or was he blissfully ignorant to everything around him because all he could focus on was whether he was going to come in his trousers?

Dan's fingers began to rub rhythmically back and forth right where I needed it most. I opened my eyes wide in alarm to try to tell him that it was too much, that I wouldn't last another minute if he did that, but he still wasn't looking at me. I concentrated on trying to make the scenario last but Dan had his own way of moving the action forwards.

'Pull her knickers down,' he said quietly, all the while looking somewhere to the side of us into the middle distance.

It was the most I could do not to come right there and then the moment I heard those words.

Armani was silent and still. I wondered whether he had heard Dan's instruction and I knew that Dan was holding his breath in anticipation, just as I was. Then both Armani's hands were holding my arse, gently kneading the flesh for a few seconds, before he hooked his fingers under my knickers and eased them over my buttocks and hips so that they came to rest halfway down my thighs. Without a moment's hesitation, Dan's fingers were inside me, filling my wetness, pushing himself deep.

I vaguely heard Armani murmur something close to my ear and then his hands were back on me, gliding over my stockings, caressing my arse, squeezing the hot flesh. And then I felt fuller still as another finger pushed inside me from behind. Together, Dan and Armani found a synchronicity that blew my mind.

I pushed myself back on Armani's fingers forcing him deeper and imagined each man's fingers touching the other's inside me, sliding through my wetness and over each other's skin as they fucked me. And that naturally led me to imagining the pair of them fucking me for real like this, their hard cocks rubbing against each other inside me. I bit my lower lip hard as Dan's thumb flicked across my clitoris, his fingers still buried deep. He held his thumb across the swelling, rocking the tip of his thumb firmly, causing exquisite stimulation.

Armani was breathing hard behind me. As I tried to hang on for just a little while longer I felt him nudge me away slightly. His fingers remained inside me but I felt his other hand move behind my arse. The movement was followed by the barely audible yet unmistakable sound of a zip unfastening. Armani's hand knocked against my arse as he worked himself to further excitement. I imagined him pulling hard, his face taut with tension, his cock ready to explode. His speed increased and the contact of his fist against my buttock became more forceful and I looked at Dan just as he withdrew his fingers from inside me and pinched my clitoris hard.

A sharp spasm of pleasure raged between my thighs and I came with such intensity that I'm sure I would have fallen down had the two men not been standing either side of me. And after a few more sporadic movements, Armani caught his breath and then became suddenly still before his body relaxed behind me.

Dan, flushed and still hard, stepped to the other side of the vestibule and breathed deeply. Armani cleared his throat and straightened his clothes. Rather touchingly, he rearranged my clothes too. I wasn't used to this post-fumble awkwardness – I never hung around that long.

The silence was broken by the train manager announcing our imminent arrival at the next station. Perfect timing. A couple of minutes sooner and we'd have had a stream of people traipsing through our little display. And perfect timing also because, when we came to a halt and a woman on the platform opened the door, my suitcase was conveniently beside me on the floor whereas Dan's was right the other end of the carriage.

'Excuse me,' I said in my sweetest voice and I picked up my luggage, pushed past an astounded Dan and stepped off the train.

I couldn't help but grin as I marched along the platform. For a moment I half expected Dan to suddenly appear beside me, panting after running to catch me up. But I knew I had been too fast for him to have realised what was happening, sped to the other end of the carriage, located his luggage and got himself off the train. I knew I had won.

I left the station and headed for the taxi rank. A taxi fare for the remainder of the journey wouldn't be cheap but seeing Dan's shocked expression had been worth it. I wondered what would be going through his mind now, stuck in the vestibule with Armani, but I didn't have the heart to be too cruel to the man who had done his utmost to accommodate my favourite kink. As I slid into the back of a cab and gave the driver the name of the Brighton hotel I sent Dan a text: 'Hope you didn't mind me getting off?'

His reply came through in seconds. 'Not at all ... so long as I'm next.'

I relaxed into my seat and smiled. I could hardly wait.

Cal Jago's short stories have been featured in numerous Wicked Words collections.

Lust for Glory
Mathilde Madden

Tuesday nights mean only one thing to Gracie, William, Mark and me: *Lust*.

Oops. Actually, that's a bit of a Freudian one – not *Lust*, *Lost*.

Lost, the TV show, that is. Every Tuesday Gracie, Mark and William pile round my place and we all watch the show. And even though we don't always follow the plot all that closely, it always, always seems to hold our attention. Mark, Gracie and William are all super hot for Doctor Jack, whereas I, not being one to follow the herd, am torn between Sawyer and Sayid. Although, I say I'm torn, but really, why choose?

We have a strict rule during *Lost* nights: no talking during *Lost*. It's complicated enough without unnecessary distractions. Not that we're that into the plot, as I said. But rules are rules and even random lustful comments have to be stored up for the ad breaks. So, because of that, tonight I've made sure that we are all sitting on the sofa with our g and ts a good twenty minutes before the show's start time, because I have something wanted to talk about: Lust.

Really, this time. Except, actually, his name is James.

*   *   *

James. A friend of William and Mark's. A very very
lovely friend indeed. I'd met James in the pub with
Mark and William about two weeks ago and I hadn't
been able to think of much else since. I was smitten.

The three of us had met up in the pub – without
Gracie – for a post mortem on a highly significant
event. Mark and William had, after months of brib-
ery, corruption and general skulduggery, managed
to get themselves a pair of invites to a very special
party. A big dirty gay party. One of the biggest and
most notorious ones anywhere, held in some big
fancy house somewhere on the South Downs.

I was, being something of a fan of Mark and
William's nefarious activities, desperate for the low-
down. I wasn't disappointed. When they described
events to me, well, 'party' seemed to be a rather
tame word for the event in question. Orgy would
have been a little more appropriate. And, big nutso
gay orgy where loads of oiled-up men writhed
around, under, over and in and out of each other
would probably have really hit the nail on the head.

Nice.

Naturally, I pumped them both mercilessly for a
full and frank account. When they gave me the
description I craved, room by room, one thing fascinated me more than any other. Sure, I loved hearing
about the orgy rooms and the dungeon and the sex
swing and the go-go boys. But none of those things
were as endlessly fascinating to me as the glory
hole.

'So, it's like, just a hole? Like, in a wall,' I said.

'Um, well –' William pouted and screwed up his
face with the supreme effort of remembering it just
right '– it's more like a big box. In this case. I think

sometimes it is a hole in a wall. Well, it can be all sorts of things, but at the party it was a big box, about five-foot square with a hole in it, like the size of this.' He held up his thumbs and forefingers, touching the tips to make a circle.

'And you just stick your...'

'You just stick your dick in it,' Mark said with a laugh.

'And someone inside...'

'Someone inside sucks it.' Mark again.

'What if they, um, what if they don't want to suck it?'

William looked at me like 'does not compute'. 'Well, the person inside, see, they're kind of in there because they *do* want to, so that doesn't really come up.'

I sighed. Fuck, but that was horny. Something about the idea of the glory hole just seemed to embody everything I found so compelling about dirty anonymous sex. The idea that men just stuck their cocks into this hole not knowing or caring who was inside to service them, spoke to a dark place inside me. And even more vividly arousing – perhaps because I don't have the required piece of anatomy to be the one sticking myself into the hole – was the thought of being the person inside, anonymously taking whatever was offered.

And then, before I really felt like the subject was exhausted, Mark shouted, 'Ooh, there's James. Hey, James.'

And this blond head at the bar turned around and, I swear, I heard birds singing. (And I don't just mean Kylie and Danni on the jukebox.)

James took my breath away. In that moment –

with the boys' salacious talk of glory holes still buzzing in the dirty part of my brain − he had it all. Beautiful, witty (OK, I found that out a bit later), single and, as Mark and William couldn't wait to point out, gay. Or in Mark's later words, 'So gay. Gay, gay, gay, gay, gay, gay, gay! Get it? Gay!'

Usually, I don't hold by those kinds of aphorism; the type of things about all the handsome men being gay or gay men taking better care of themselves. That stuff. I reckon all that is just made up to make women feel bad. And, me, I'm not that big a fan of feeling bad. Not when there are so many other great ways to feel. However, it was very true that James was both handsome and gay. Very handsome and very gay. ('Gay, gay, gay, gay, gay, gay, gay!', in fact, let us not forget.) And I wanted him nasty bad.

William and Mark − I should point out − I didn't want. Still don't want. Even though there really would have been no problem there, because William and Mark weren't so much gay as sexually gluttonous. A pair of dirtier boys I had never yet met. Sometimes I thought that Mark was probably properly bi, and William was mostly gay but open to opportunity, but I never really figured it out. Needless to say though, our combined dirtiness (dirty to the power of three) was probably the cement that held our friendship together. But we never took all the frisson and flirting into the bedroom. There was a line. An unwritten rule. It never quite went that far. Although, actually I'm pretty sure it spilt over into the bedroom between Mark and William, but not between me and either of them. (Well, OK, I'd snogged them both. Separately. But what girl hasn't snogged her gay(ish) male mates? Just as an experiment.)

But I'd always insisted that Mark and William were just my fag bangles. Or maybe I was theirs. I never quite figured out how that term was meant to go.

But anyway, after two weeks of obsessing about delicious James, I decide enough is enough. Nothing ventured and all that. So making sure I've got a good ten minutes before *Lust*-I-mean-*Lost* starts I tell William and Mark and Gracie of my enduring passion.

'Angel,' William says, after I outline my angst, 'James is gay. Forget it.'

'But, but, but,' I say, stalling for time while I wait for something to appear in my brain. 'But he might be one of those gay guys who sleep with women.' *Rather like the two I'm looking at right now.*

'He isn't.'

'But he might want to sleep with a woman just once, just to check he doesn't like it.'

Mark shakes his head. 'If – and that's a giant-size "if" with flashing neon lights on the top – he did want to do that, he probably would have done it by now.'

'But he might just not have met the right woman yet.'

'I'll pretend I didn't hear that,' William says, raising his eyebrows so high they almost wrap around the back of his forehead.

I scrabble around for some chance I might get my way. 'But, well, couldn't I convert him? I hear you and your friends boasting about converting straight guys all the time. What's that joke? "What's the difference between a straight guy and a gay guy?", "About five pints of lager." Couldn't it work the other way? Can you turn gay boys straight with enough alcohol?'

'No,' William and Mark say, both at once and snappily fast.

'But couldn't I just suck his cock? I mean, what difference would it make?' I say hopefully, my James fantasies suddenly clashing with my glory hole fantasies and almost overloading my brain.

'What?' Again they both speak together. It's like they have become one consciousness.

'What difference would it make if I were a guy or a girl then? I have a mouth, right?' I insist.

'Babe,' says Mark, 'cock-sucking is an art, perfected by gay men over the millennia. There is no way you could suck cock as well as a gay guy.'

'Actually, I'm pretty good at sucking cock,' I say, because actually, I am. I enjoy it. Over the years I've made it my business to be good at it. I know some women don't like it, but I don't get that, what's not to like? What else has the same twisted conflicting rush of being empowered by being able to give such incredible pleasure while at the same time being used and degraded? It ticks all the boxes.

Mark gives me a yeah-right kind of look.

'He'd never even know the difference,' I say, quite softly.

William shakes his head. 'It doesn't work like that. I mean, you're not just talking about James getting his rocks off. You're talking about a person's political, social and sexual identity. You're talking about light years of repression.'

'Light years is a measure of distance, not time,' Mark points out, unhelpfully.

'But if he *thinks* I'm a guy, what difference does it make?'

And then Gracie, who has been very quiet throughout this debate says, 'It's starting,' and I have to shut up for ten whole minutes until the first ad break.

I don't get to set the conversational agenda to me, me, me in the first ad break because Gracie says, 'Do any of you lot want to earn some extra spending money this weekend?'

Gracie runs her own sort of company. Sort of. It's basically a catering company, but she likes to pretend they do events management and party planning as well. They don't. They reheat vol-au-vents and serve champagne. And it's not really even a proper company because Gracie's family are utterly loaded and the entire organisation is being propped up by the generous handouts her family keep giving her (supposedly to avoid paying inheritance tax).

I don't like working for Gracie at the weekend. For any number of reasons born of both laziness and class-warring principle, but she does pay pretty well and I've been a bit trigger happy on eBay lately – my last credit card bill was just a piece of paper with the words 'Oh my fucking God' written on it.

'Front of house?' I ask, because wafting around topping up champagne glasses is slightly better than unloading and reloading a dishwasher in an ancient kitchen.

Gracie winces. 'Front for Willy or Markie, back for you, Lou.'

'What? Why?'

'Um, well, it's kind of a men-only kind of party,' Gracie says and makes such a weird face that you would actually think she couldn't possibly conceive of why a group of men would want to have a private party with no women around. Her. Her who is sitting here next to Mark and William. William with his hand down the front of Mark's trousers – I swear he's giving him a little squeeze every time the good doctor appears on screen.

Then William says, 'Um, I don't think I can make this weekend, sorry.'

He and Mark exchanges glances. And then Mark says, 'No, nor can I.'

'Lou?' Gracie says to me. I'm still feeling a bit pissed off about having to be behind closed doors. It's a bit much that I have come off badly purely because of my gender twice in the space of half an hour. But I think of that credit card bill again and shrug my shoulders. 'Sure.'

In the next ad break Gracie goes to the loo and I say to William, 'This is going to be one of *those* parties, isn't it?'

'One of what parties?'

'One of those dirty parties. Like you told me about in the pub. The plushie orgies?'

'Oh.' William nods. 'Oh, yes.'

Mark says, 'Actually you do know "plushie" means something very specific. You should watch you terminology there, girl.'

But I ignore Mark's sexual semantics lesson. 'So how come you're not going?' I ask both of them.

William gives me a look. 'Who says we're not going?' he says, with emphasis.

Then, when Gracie returns and *Lost* starts up again, I find I'm not really paying attention to the show any more, despite the delicious parade of prettiness dancing across the screen – and I don't mean Hawaii.

Four days later it's party time. Except not for me. The work on Saturday afternoon is hard. The house itself is stunning, a real country pile, all huge stone steps and crunchy gravel drive. Not that I'm seeing much of that. I'm strictly below stairs.

My job seems to be mostly washing up baking trays in a huge Belfast sink which screams whenever the taps are run and refuses to supply me with water any more than a few degrees above room temperature. That and running around fetching things.

It's hard to decide which is worst really.

At about six thirty the grumpier of the two chefs (not that the other one isn't grumpy) yells at me that we haven't got any fresh basil, and before I can respond that that is hardly my fault, Gracie appears and apologetically explains that a tray of fresh herbs seems to have gone missing and could I possibly run round to the front door of the house and find out if it got delivered there by mistake.

I nip out of the kitchen door and sprint around the side of the massive house. It's further than I would have thought possible. When I get there, there's about twenty cars parked on the drive, but no one around.

I look around hopefully, wondering if I will see a tray of herbs that has been tucked neatly by the door, like the postman sometimes does with my eBay parcels if they won't fit the letterbox.

But nothing.

And then I notice the front door is actually just a little bit open. Which makes me think that maybe I could cut through the house and get back to the kitchen that way rather than go around the outside. Not very upstairs downstairs, I know, but I'm pretty eager for a sneaky peak at the dirty party set-up.

Inside the house isn't the riot of tapestries and old masters I might have imagined from its façade. It's kind of like an ordinary house really, only on a more massive and massively kinky scale. Just the entrance hall I am standing in contains a bank of man-sized cages, a set of stocks and a huge over-flowing bowl of condoms.

As I walk through this den of iniquity I stop by the condom bowl. Something has caught my magpie eye. Right in the centre of it is a gold condom. Hardly the most spectacular thing in the room, but strangely compelling. It holds my gaze. And then I reach out and grab it.

But as I do that, I realise that there is the soft sound of conversation coming from the room on my left. I go over and peek through an ajar door into a gorgeous ballroom. And it's full of people. Men. Most of them naked, semi-naked or wearing various exotica. *Oh my God, the party has already started.* I stare around the entrance hall. Frozen. And then I hear it. Footsteps. Someone is coming up the steps outside, any minute now they're going to be coming in the front door. I don't know what to do. I dart behind the bank of cages and leg it up the imposing staircase behind me.

I try to make my way back to the kitchens as best as I can, keeping a look out in case I bump into any party guests. But the upstairs part of the house seems deserted. Maybe the party hasn't really begun properly yet. I still manage to take a few wrong turnings though. Get lost. Get double lost. Try to retrace my steps. Fail. Double back again and find I am utterly, well, lost. Real life being lost – nothing like as fun as the TV show. I can't even find my way back to the front entrance. Desperate, I head up another flight of stairs.

But being further upstairs doesn't seem to be proving any better for finding my way out. Damn my retarded sense of direction. I just seem to be winding my way deeper into the house.

Here the party-in-waiting becomes something rather darker than the almost light-hearted bondage fun downstairs. Upstairs, most rooms are dark, in half-light or freakily strobe lit. The background music has changed from twinkly classical to throbbing German industrial.

I glance into a medium-sized room, which is mostly empty. All it contains is a heavy red velvet curtain, through which peeks a large wooden box, with a hole in it. A really very large wooden box with a rather small hole in it. Of course, I know exactly what it is. And I know I shouldn't, but I can't resist a closer look.

But before I get even halfway across the room towards it, a voice behind me says, 'Excuse me.' And

I turn around to find if not the last person I would have expected, certainly a double-take-worthy coincidence.

'William?'

'Lou. Hey.'

'Um ... I got lost,' I say, feeling a bit awkward. 'What are you doing here?'

'Well, I kind of told you I might be here.'

'Yeah, but what are you doing *here*? Shouldn't you be downstairs?'

And then William starts to look shiftily at the box, and I follow his gaze with one of those dawning revelation feelings. 'Oh.' I point across the room. 'You're meant to be in *there*.'

But before I can say anything else, a tinny tune strikes up from somewhere in William's pocket. 'Woah,' he says. 'Girl, interrupted.' And fishes in the pocket of his tight, tight jeans for a phone that is playing the theme to *Bewitched*. 'Yep. Mark, hey dude,' he twitters into it.

I look over at the box while he's talking. Thinking about what he told me about the glory hole. Feeling myself get buzzy and wet with the filthy idea of it.

And I suppose I'm lost in all of that, which means I don't notice the way things have changed in William's voice. The way most of his phone conversation is being punctuated by angry and frustrated swearing. 'Fuck!' says William. And then again, 'Fuck!' as he hangs up the phone.

'Something wrong?'

'That stupid fairy Mark's only gone and locked himself out. I'm going to have to drive back to Brighton with my keys and sort it.'

'What? Isn't Mark here?'

'No, he's revising. He's got an exam in the morning. Hence me having to go and let him back in. All his notes are in the flat.'

'But didn't you tell him you were kind of busy?' I tip my head towards the box, which is making its presence felt like a third person in the room.

'Yeah, but, oh God. What can I do? Look, it'll only take three-quarters of an hour, max. I'll just find someone else to take my place for a bit. James is downstairs maybe he would –'

'James is downstairs!'

'Yeah.' William blinks at me, like he's thinking, why is that surprising?

I'm still holding the little gold foil packet in my hand. I rub my fingers across it like a lucky charm. 'I'll do it,' I say.

At first William looks at me like I've just said something in a foreign language. 'You? You can't.'

'Why not? No one'll know. Go on, William, you can sneak out. No one'll even know it wasn't you in there all night.'

William puffs out his slim chest. 'Oh, you still reckon you can suck cock as well as a gay boy, do you?'

'Sure. How hard can it be?' I say, turning to walk over to the box, not looking back at William, just hoping he'll follow me.

'You are such a dirty bitch,' he says, appearing right at my shoulder, and my heart leaps.

I don't reply. I push aside the heavy velvet curtain that the box protrudes from. And once we are 'backstage' I see exactly how it works.

The box has no back to it. So it's more like a sort of cubbyhole. Inside it is a small firm cushion for the person inside the box to kneel on. And if a person were kneeling on that cushion, facing the wooden wall of the box, the small hole would be at about face height. In fact, to be really strictly accurate, it would be at mouth height.

Still not speaking, feeling the tension in the air, I drop onto my knees. Oh God, the buzz hits me straight away.

I look over my shoulder at William. He has an odd expression on his face. 'Are you really OK with this?' I ask, not really knowing what I'll say if he tells me he isn't.

'I don't know,' he says, biting his bottom lip. 'It's just, it's not very ethical, is it?'

'I guess not. But then, when did you last worry about ethics when it came to sex? I mean, you're always joking about getting straight guys drunk and shagging them.'

'Yeah, but that's just a fantasy, Lou. I don't actually do it.'

'You don't?'

'No!'

'Oh.' I look at William for quite a long time then, so long I actually start to worry about Mark and his revision timetable. 'Are you really not OK with this?'

William seems to have a change of heart then, because he sort of micro-smirks and then says, 'Nah, not really. Well, except that I'm worried that after this everyone will think I can't suck cock for toffee. Do you want the cuffs?'

'What!' I sort of splutter, because that really blindsided me. 'Cuffs?'

'Yes, uh, some people like to be, uh . . .' William's

voice kind of drains away along with the colour in his face.

It's weird. William and I are really close. Tight. I'm closer to William than I am to Mark. I could tell William anything, despite his occasional screams of 'Ooh, you breeders!' Which is a bit rich really seeing as how William is all for a bit of heterosexual action when he can get it. Really, he reserves that squeal for when I tell him about something a little too risqué even for him. I've always been the slightly more adventurous one out of the three of us, which, I think, he sees as upsetting the natural order of things. But, see me kneeling in a glory-hole box at a gay orgy right now for details of my spirit of sexual derring-do.

However, despite all of that, all that sexual camaraderie, this is maybe a bit too far. That line I talked about – the one that stops us all sleeping together. It's here too. Drawn across the sand. The idea of William putting the cuffs on me. A bit too much. But I really want them. So I have to screw up every ounce of my sexual courage to say, 'Actually, yes. That would be good.'

While I kneel in the box, my knees quite comfortable on the soft padding and my lips just a breath away from the ominous hole, William straps my wrists together behind my back with something that feels firm and restrictive and comfortable all at once. I can't help sighing while he does it. It feels so good. So right.

I'm not really very with it when William says, 'OK, Lou, I've really got to go now. Mark, etc.'

'Yeah, um, before you do though, I need a favour.'

'*Another* one?'

'Yeah, look, take the condom that's in my pocket. I want you to give it to James.'

'To James, why?'

'Just do it.'

William is actually quite well behaved as he roots around in the pocket of my jeans for the condom while my hands are tied. When he snags it and leaves, with a gentle goodbye of a finger trailing on my shoulder, my heart is banging like a drum and my clit is throbbing in perfect time with it.

My lips suddenly feel dry. I lick them in anticipation. Then I wait.

For quite while nothing actually happens. I listen to the faint thrum of the Rammstein playing in the hall and wonder if anyone will actually come and use the box, feeling faintly disappointed that I'm not much of an attraction.

After, I guess, five minutes though, I hear sounds in the room outside and without any warning I feel the unmistakable soft force of a rubber-coated cock pressing against my suddenly dry lips. I open my mouth and suck.

God, it feels amazing. Hard to explain. The anonymity. The bondage. And the fact that the room on the other side of the wooden wall is now full of people. That unique mix of power and subjugation is like a head rush. I use every wile I have. Every last trick of lips and teeth. When my mystery man comes, he groans loudly and falls against the wood so hard it shakes.

One down.

There's another hard cock jutting through the hole before I even draw breath.

I open up my mouth again for the next one, cutely jacketed in bright blue and, as I do so, I tug a little at the restraints holding my hands behind my back. God, it turns me on not to be able to use my hands while I'm being used like this. It makes everything so much more arousing.

My clit is burning as I let the new cock force its way inside and jerk roughly in my mouth. This guy is much more forceful. He doesn't let me play artful games, but thrusts hard through the hole. In and out. Fucking my mouth. I hold still and let him. Squirming with pleasure when I hear a distinct and masterful snarl.

Three follows, then four, then five. My wrists get sore, and my jaw starts to ache, and my cunt gets wetter and wetter.

I've just finished number six, when I start to wonder where the hell William has got to. I can't see my watch so I don't know how long I've been here. There's a part of me that's worried, but a bigger part that, despite my aching neck and jaw, kind of hopes he never comes back.

And then – lucky number seven – in through the hole comes what I've been waiting for. And I'm going for gold.

I pause for a moment to look at it. It's beautiful. The last part of James that I get to study in depth is every bit as pleasing to behold as the rest of him. It's so big and thick. I never knew I was a size queen, but James doesn't disappoint on that score. He's going to be more than a mouthful.

He's also got this little kink in his cock. It bends over to the left. It's nice. It's quirky. Makes it more real – him not being dildo straight and perfect. It doesn't hurt that the whole thing is clad in golden rubber either. I pause maybe a moment too long looking at its golden glory, because there's a knock on the wooden wall above my head.

James. I open my mouth and suck.

James's big hard cock is filling my mouth, thrusting hard, mercilessly using me. I can hear some faint groaning coming from the other side of the wall. *Him.* Too faint to recognise, but it's got to be him. I'm so wet, my clit feels like it's burning. I tug at the restraints that hold my wrist, both frustrated and fiercely aroused by not being able to touch myself. As James keeps on going, holding out for longer than anyone else has tonight under my cock-sucking prowess, I squeeze my thighs together. Over and over, setting up a strong pulsing rhythm. I squirm around on the cushion, ignoring the protests from my sore knees and find a way to get the pressure on my clit just right, even without my hands. I concentrate on the way James is forcing his way right down my throat, the way my lips are stretching around him, going numb. The way he has no idea that it is me, William's friend, so quickly dismissed, that is making him feel this intense pleasure.

James starts to move faster, jerking like he's not in control. I suck as hard as I can, using my tongue to massage the underside of his shaft. I squeeze my thighs harder together. Twist a little. Feel the pressure just right and there it is. James is spasming hotly under his rubber sleeve and I'm coming so hard I don't know which way is up.

I don't know if I could have taken another cock after that. So thank God that the hole goes dark for a minute or two after James withdraws.

And then I hear a sound behind me, and look over my shoulder to see William, reaching over to unfasten my wrists.

'Bloody hell, William, you've been ages.'

'I've been less than an hour.'

'Well, it seemed like longer.' I pull my arms free, struggling to move, not knowing what part of me to massage first. I scarcely even get my wits together before William practically yanks me out of the box, through a side door behind the curtain and directs me down a flight of stairs to the kitchen.

Gracie looks up as I walk in, tottering gingerly like I am eighty years old. 'I'm not even going to ask,' she says as I collapse into a chair. 'But if you think you're getting paid for today ...'

I'm not listening.

A couple of hours later I try to make amends to Gracie. My body feels rather more alive after two gin and tonics and about a hundred vol-au-vents. My jaw actually does still work, despite early reports of it completely seizing up. Flaky pastry has brought it back to life. Eventually I struggle over to the pre-war dishwasher and start loading champagne glasses in and out, all the time feeling hot flares at the memory of James and his spectacular cock in my mouth. *Oh yeah.*

* * *

At about 1 a.m. this guy called Sebastian, apparently the host of the party although it's the first I've seen of him, appears in the kitchen to slather us with congratulations. Either it's gone extremely well or he is extremely pissed – possibly both. Sebastian invites Gracie, me, the chefs and Gracie's other galley slaves up to the hall for a final drink. I raise my eyebrows at Gracie because of the whole no-women thing, and she just mimes 'too much to drink' with an invisible glass to her lips.

In the hall, I approach William, who almost jumps out of his skin. 'Hey, Lou, what you doing up here?'

'Heh. We've been allowed above stairs. Where's James?'

'Um.' Suddenly William looks awfully shifty.

'Has he gone home?'

'Uh, yeah. That's it, yeah, he's gone home. Busy day tomorrow or something.' Which would be perfectly plausible if it weren't for the look on William's face.

But I don't worry about that too much. 'Oh, right. Did he say anything about my blow job? Best ever, right?'

But before William can answer me, someone appears at his shoulder. Someone who changes everything.

'Hey, Lou,' says Mark.

William glares. 'Mark.'

'Mark. What are you doing here? I thought you were at home, revising?' Two and two are rapidly making four in my head.

'Um . . . Oh,' says Mark, reddening a bit.

'But you're not, are you?' I say to Mark, then turn

to William. 'So you didn't have to go and let him into his flat, did you?'

'Uh.'

'Did you?'

'No.' William looks at his shoes. But he's smirking.

'So, what? You set me up. Why?' And then something else dawns on me as I cast around the room. 'James was never even here, was he? I thought it was weird. I thought he didn't seem the type.'

Mark and William look bashfully at me. Then Mark says, 'He *was* here.'

I shake my head. 'Don't lie.'

'It's true,' says William. 'He was, but he's gone now.' They're both smirking. I honestly don't know if they're lying or not.

'OK, well, was it him then? Was he the one with the gold condom on?'

William reaches out and touches my shoulder. 'Well, honey,' he says gently, 'the fact is, you *thought* it was him. So really, what difference does it make?'

Mathilde Madden is the author of the Black Lace novels *Peep Show*, *Mad About the Boy*, and *Equal Opportunities*.

Montague Heights Toni Sands

'Well, do you want the job, or not?' said Maz.

I watched, fascinated, as she inserted a chocolate flake bar between her glossy lips, her tongue lapping at the tiny particles. 'Doesn't the client want to interview me first?' I asked. The apartment was in Montague Heights, the ritziest address in the city.

'He trusts my judgement,' said Maz. 'And he's asked for a trial period of one month either side. He's in now, so why don't you get over there and finalise details? He'll pay your taxi fare.'

'Sounds too good to be true,' I said.

Maz shrugged. 'For a cleaning job, it's good money. Though I wish you'd let us find you a secretarial position.' Her brown eyes appraised my body. 'With your skills you could get a top PA job.' She handed me an envelope. 'For your new boss,' she said.

I needed to earn some money, having returned to the UK after working in New York for five years. And yes, of course, I'd split up with someone. I was in no hurry to saddle myself with another high-powered job where the only people I met were workaholics. I'd been there and done that. I might pick up a few hours' glamour modelling or whatever. I'd done that before too.

Montague Heights had its own doorman. When I explained whom I'd come to see he told me to go up in the lift. I was curious about the man I'd be working for. He was probably a rich old buffer who made a ritual of his Earl Grey tea and cucumber sandwiches.

But when the door opened, the guy standing there didn't look a day over forty. He had cropped black hair flecked with silvery grey and a crumpled ugly-attractive sort of face. He went on talking into his mobile phone as he beckoned me in. On the way to the sitting room I noticed display cabinets filled with beautiful china and breathtakingly delicate glass. Some of the paintings looked like they cost a fortune too. Thick cream and amber rugs floated on the pale wood floors. Gold drapes shimmered against the parchment walls.

He finished his call. 'Sit down, please. It's Miss or Mrs . . .?'

I passed him Maz's envelope before sinking onto a flame velvet chesterfield. 'It's Ms Delahaye. Tessa Delahaye, Mr Cole.'

He read the A4 sheet without once glancing at me. When he finished it, he tossed it aside.

'You don't appear to have much cleaning experience,' he said.

'I lived for five years with a complete slob,' I said.

'You're over-qualified for this job,' he said.

'Can I help it if I'm a domestic goddess with a brain?'

'Can you start now?' he asked.

'I'd work better if I'd eaten lunch,' I said.

'Fix me a sandwich and you can eat here,' he said.

'You're on,' I said.

On seeing that kitchen, any domestic goddess would have thought she'd died and gone to heaven.

Mr Cole was on the phone constantly while I prepared the snack. I found French bread, smoked salmon, lemons and, yes, cucumber. Judging by the amount of mineral water chilling, I figured a glass of sparkling volcanic wouldn't go amiss. I put the tray in front of him as he was shouting down the phone at some poor devil and he totally ignored me. Charming. With any luck he wouldn't be around much and if he were too obnoxious, I'd find something else.

My new boss came in when I was just finishing my sandwich. He walked over to the espresso machine. 'Coffee?' he asked.

'Thank you,' I said. 'Would you like me to make it?'

'I'm OK,' he said. 'Lunch was good.'

'I had the right materials,' I said. 'If you don't mind my asking, don't you need to hire a housekeeper rather than a cleaning lady?'

His lips twitched. 'Do you have a cleaning fetish to tell me about?' he asked. 'I was hoping you'd prepare the odd snack, iron the occasional shirt when you're not on your knees scrubbing the quarry tiles with a toothbrush.'

I couldn't help but laugh at him. He was a rough diamond but one with such style that I began to feel sorry I hadn't met him in a social context. But no doubt there was a sweet little wife in green wellies waiting with her knickers off by the Aga, in Wiltshire or somewhere.

'You'll be well paid for any duties you don't regard as being within your remit, Tessa,' he said. 'And I would appreciate it if you'd wear a uniform whilst you are at work. You can purchase some high-necked black overalls. I can't stand cardigans and leggings and baggy T-shirts. It's more professional for both of us if there's a dress code.'

I was wearing a navy-blue trouser suit with a jade-green camisole under the fitted jacket. I looked pointedly at him then lowered my eyes towards my outfit. He looked sheepish and shuffled his feet a bit. Got him. He handed me a cup of coffee.

'Yes. Yes ... well, I'm sorry, Tessa. You will of course be reimbursed for the uniform. Just give all your expense claims to that agency woman.' He looked at his watch. 'I have to go. Can you find whatever you need? Just buy stuff if it's not already there. And before I forget...' He handed me a door key. 'Twenty hours a week, all right?' he called over his shoulder.

I poured the remains of his coffee down the sink. The flat was quiet without him but I told myself not to be so stupid. To afford a pad like this, he obviously had better things to do than sit at home in his slippers.

I toured the apartment and found that the master bedroom overlooked the park. I admired the view, watching a rider in the distance, his butt bobbing up and down in its tight jodhpurs. The en suite facilities were less than pristine so I decided there was no time like the present. I'd do a couple of hours to make a good impression then go and buy my uniform like a good girl on the way home.

Not wishing to mess up my clothes, I took off my jacket and slipped out of my boots and trousers. Cleaning his bathroom took me almost an hour.

Poor Mr Cole must have been without domestic help for quite some while, I thought. I hoped that didn't mean he was a difficult boss.

I was singing my favourite Kylie song and wiggling my butt from side to side as I polished the bath so I didn't hear the boss let himself into the flat and enter the bedroom.

'Jeez,' he said.

I almost jumped out of my skin. His gaze was riveted on my flesh-coloured panties so I folded my rubber-gloved hands demurely in front of me. At least my top half was covered.

'I've got to fly to Glasgow,' he said. 'I'll be away a night or two so I need to pack.'

'Just give me a moment,' I said. 'Then, if you want me to, I'll help you, if you hand me your clothes.'

'Thank you,' he said, handing me my trousers.

'I promise to be in my domestic uniform next time you see me, sir,' I said primly. 'I just had to make a start on your en suite facilities.'

I was surprised how sexy I felt in my little black number. It was tight enough over the hips for my panty line to show through when I was standing in the wrong light. And I had to keep the top two or four buttons undone in order to work comfortably. Sheer black tights looked better with the flat black pumps I'd bought for work. After all, the boss wouldn't want me grinding my stilettos into those blond floors and sumptuous rugs.

My auburn hair looked good against the black, especially after I twisted it into a severe pleat. At least I looked the part now. If I could just get some sort of working routine sorted, everything should go well. It was a big apartment to look after in twenty hours a week.

I worked for five hours for each of the days Mr C. was in Scotland. It was surprisingly satisfying seeing dusty surfaces left shining in my wake. I couldn't see myself making a career out of housekeeping though. The surroundings were luxurious but I was a bit lonely. That's why my insides lurched the next day when I heard the boss's key in the lock.

'Tessa, could you make some coffee, please?' He sounded exhausted. I heard him playing back his answerphone messages. When I took the coffee through, he was sitting in a big leather recliner chair, tie loosened and shoes off. Then he looked up at me.

I hadn't actually acknowledged to myself what was really going on when I was tarting myself up in the housekeeper uniform. I only hoped I hadn't gone over the top because he seemed lost for words when I bent down to pick up the pen he'd dropped. Those granite eyes darkened even more as he watched my breasts spilling out of my black overall.

'Thanks,' he said. 'Everything under control I take it? I haven't had a chance to, um, explore yet but you seem to have made a big difference already.'

I nodded. The bulge at his groin was certainly a big difference. 'How did your trip go?' I asked.

'It went,' he said. He began leafing through his briefcase so I took the hint and returned to my chores. But I could feel his eyes following my progress back to the kitchen. I leaned against the state-of-the-art fridge-freezer. I could swear my knickers were damp. So much for a relationship-free break and no career hassles – I should have gone to work in Waitrose. They had smart uniforms too.

For the rest of my shift I kept out of the way. I was aware of him going into his bedroom and firmly shutting the door. Maybe he was unzipping his trousers, groaning as he released his erect cock to begin pumping it. Or, maybe he was taking a cold shower. I pictured him stripped naked, soaping his long lean frame, hands rubbing the suds into his groin, the water spurting down his thighs. I forced myself to concentrate. Towels, I thought. Towels from the airing cupboard to replace the ones he'll use. But my disobedient mind was rerunning the scenario and I imagined holding out a soft, fluffy bath sheet so he could walk into my arms and allow me to pat and rub every inch of his dripping body till he was dry.

I realised my knickers really were damp. I was the one who needed a cold shower. Maybe I should buy the domestic operative's book of etiquette to see how to conduct myself. I certainly shouldn't be going round lusting after my boss all the time he was in the apartment.

But the next day when he was out during my stint, it was almost worse than his being in residence. His smell lingered in the bathroom and on the towel he'd used after shaving. His cologne was a blend of musk, lime and leather that was pure sex in a bottle. And I really knew I was becoming depraved when I found some jet-black pubic hairs in the walk-in shower and started feeling turned on. I prowled around his bedroom like a lioness on heat.

He wasn't a pyjama man. No surprise there. There were no glossy girly magazines in evidence, just one hefty paperback novel. There were no signs of any feminine occupation. I'd checked out the other bedrooms and the guest bathroom and there wasn't even a stray toothbrush. He kept one cupboard locked. It probably contained his personal documents.

We had no fixed routine for my visits. I always rang the bell and waited before inserting my key in the lock. Just once or twice he'd come and let me in, then gone back to make more phone calls or sit in front of his computer. We met briefly in passing or when I made coffee and he would ask me how I was. We were both on our best behaviour. And my uniform was always immaculate.

It was like being in the company of a huge, powerful tiger, being around this guy. He was taut and trim and I knew he ran in the mornings and swam lengths once or twice a week at a local pool. He ate out a lot and he liked me to keep the fridge well stocked with freshly ground coffee and luxury food to graze on.

He seemed to go away at weekends. He was no doubt a faithful husband, which would of course explain his low profile with women. I wondered what the country pad was like and whether his wife ever ventured into the city to shop or to take in a show.

I took the opportunity to find out if he was going away the following weekend when he asked me to prepare him a salad on the Thursday lunchtime. I'd been in my job for almost three weeks.

'Haven't decided yet,' he said. 'There's paperwork to catch up on but I suppose I should take a break.'

I held my breath. 'I expect your wife will miss

you if you don't go home,' I said, brushing a long scarlet radish against my lips before I popped it into my mouth.

He looked at me with those granite eyes of his and shrugged. 'She's used to me,' he said.

I knew better than to push him further.

I fully admit it was wrong of me. It wasn't at all professional and I deserved to lose my job over it but I had this fantasy and I was pining for it to come true. So, early on the Saturday evening, having rung the apartment and got the answerphone, I took the bus to Montague Heights. It was dusk and a quick glance up at Mr C's windows on the first floor showed no lights. Joe the doorman was on duty but he was so used to me by now that he just gave me a quick wave, calling across, 'What's this, love, overtime?'

I waved back, about to blurt out that I'd agreed to do some bulk cooking for Mr Cole's freezer but Joe just tapped the side of his nose and gave me an exaggerated wink. I hadn't a clue what he meant but his phone rang so I escaped into the lift.

When I stood outside the door to the apartment I rang the bell, just in case. I had an excuse all ready in the event that the boss might be in residence after all but it appeared I was safe. He must have gone home to the country. I let myself in and switched a couple of lamps on. The heating was on a timer and the apartment felt warm and welcoming. So it was no hardship to take my clothes off.

I'd put a bottle of Chardonnay to chill the day before and I sipped my wine from a crystal goblet as I walked from room to room, sneaking glances at my naked body in every mirror. I let my toes burrow into the deep pile of the carpet when I reached the master bedroom. The scent of the lilies I had arranged in the hall the day before drifted into the room, mingling with the fruity taste of the wine.

I was in the walk-in shower, blatantly rubbing Harrods's blissful bath gel on the loofah when I sensed rather than heard a door close. I turned around, my heart pounding, uncertain as to what I should do. Who else had a key? Nobody appeared and those moments of anxiety felt like an eternity as I waited, uncertain whether to reach for the towel or stay where I was. Then he was there. Our eyes met and I could see the uncertainty in his, softening to relief as he saw me. His gaze shifted to my boobs and then wandered lower still. Neither of us said a word. It's difficult to know what to say when you're naked in your boss's shower and he's fully clothed and probably in shock. Then his eyes met mine again and I knew what I had to do.

Following my instincts, I moved both my hands to cup my breasts. Relief flooded me as he undid the belt of his black jeans, peeled them off and then ripped off his sweater and T-shirt. His designer underpants were having trouble trying to contain his deliciously precocious cock as it pointed in my direction.

The shower was more than big enough for two and we took turns soaping each other in imaginative ways. His touch was gentle where it should be and firm in the other places.

'Your nipples are standing out like raspberries against the cream of your skin,' he whispered against my ear when at last he turned off the spray.

The tip of his tongue lingered in my ear, lapping at the folds like a gourmet freeing an oyster from its shell.

I shivered and brushed my hand against his erection. 'You can't have the dessert before the main course,' I said.

He picked up a towel and wound it round his waist. Then he began patting me dry, so gently and carefully that I don't know how I managed to stand there. 'You're a very naughty girl,' he murmured as he dried the tops of my thighs without once touching my bush, the bastard. He certainly knew what he was doing. I was as taut as the strings on a tennis pro's racquet when he finished drying himself, never taking his gaze from my eyes.

'I can explain,' I said, trying to remember the excuse I'd cooked up to explain this invasion of his privacy. I had enacted my fantasy so many times. When you're sharing a flat that's a tip and your three flatmates bring their boyfriends back on Saturday nights, the thought of the Montague Heights apartment with its peace and lush décor becomes an oasis in the middle of the desert.

'Shall I put some clothes on?' My question was one that Mr C didn't immediately answer. He didn't seem to want an explanation as to my conduct either.

'I wish you'd put your black uniform on again,' he said. 'So I can unbutton it.'

'How do you know I wore my uniform to come here tonight?' I asked.

'I saw it on the bed − you left the door to the blue bedroom ajar. I picked up your uniform and smelled your perfume and imagined how you would look

without it on and then I walked into the bathroom
and there you were. I would have gone away again
if you'd panicked at the sight of me but then you
held your gorgeous tits up for me and I knew you
wanted me just as much as I wanted you. Is that
right, Tessa? I hope it is.'

It was the longest speech I'd ever heard him
make. I walked across to the bed and picked up my
panties. I held them under his nostrils just fleetingly
so he could smell my scent before I stepped into
them. I fastened my bra, leaning towards him so he
could watch the twin globes bulge and settle into
the lacy cups. Then I put on my black uniform and
did up every single button, starting from the top.

Mr C looked like a little boy staring at a display
of sweets. When I sat down on the bed and pulled
on sheer black lacy hold-up stockings, he swallowed
hard. But I wasn't going to get my hands on his
lollipop yet.

'I'll fix us a drink,' he said. 'Stay there a moment.'

I waited, taking deep breaths because I was desperate to touch myself and would do so if he didn't
do something very soon. But there was more tor-
ment to come. Didn't I say he had style?

I heard him call to me from outside the door. 'I'd
like to speak to you in the sitting room please, Ms
Delahaye.'

So that was how he wanted to play it? I could go
along with that. I walked through to join him. He
was standing in front of the mantelpiece with his
glass in his hand. My drink was on the coffee table
in front of the chesterfield.

'Sit down, please,' he said, 'and enjoy your wine.
But I'm afraid I need to demonstrate to you that you

really have been a naughty girl. What if I'd brought a woman home and we'd found you here? What if I had brought a business colleague back and surprised you? And, whatever must Joe the doorman be thinking?'

I kept my eyes downcast. I crossed one leg over the other so he could see up my skirt to the band of bare flesh between lacy stocking top and panties. I sipped at my Chardonnay again. Then I raised my head and let the tip of my tongue peep through my parted lips before I answered in my best breathy voice, 'I think I deserve a spanking.'

'Come here then,' he said.

I got up and walked towards him, biting the tip of my index finger. My hair hung in damp tendrils around my face. He groaned and pulled me onto his lap, with some difficulty however. He used the back of a hairbrush though I'd been anticipating he'd have some sort of paddle or maybe horsetail whip. I soon realised he knew something about chastising because the smacking was not painful but hard enough to be arousing and I cried out with pleasure as the sweet sting of the brush made contact with my buttocks through the taut fabric of my overall. Lying across his thighs, I came and I came beautifully, even wetting my knickers.

'Clever girl,' he said softly. 'You deserve a treat now you've been punished.'

We stood up together and he undid the buttons on my black uniform, starting at the hem and working his way up. By the time he reached the top one, his cock was grazing my panties and he wasn't standing too close to me either. I was wet, licking my lips at the thought of the treat in store as he pushed my knickers down. He was tall and fit enough to fit his shaft inside me and support me with his hands cupping my bottom so we stood locked together, his whole length filling me while I pushed my tongue in and out of his warm, wet mouth. This time, when I came, I cried out. But his self-control was awesome.

'You're a joy,' he said, smiling at me. 'You just love it, don't you? Come on – let's see if we can make it even better for you. I want to show you something.'

He took my hand and pulled me after him like a damp pulsating little tug. We went into his bedroom and he took a tiny gold key from his bedside drawer and walked over to the big cupboard.

'I've been shopping on the internet,' he explained as he pulled something out of the cupboard that sent shivers up and down my spine. I had to admire the riding bench's workmanship with its rich upholstery of dark-plum leather. As I watched Mr C's long fingers stroking the curved saddle, I imagined the power of his strong thighs as they gripped the leather, his feet imprisoned in the stirrups while he rode behind me.

I was already wet but Mr C pushed me back onto his king-sized bed and produced some delicious-smelling otion. He lightly massaged around my clitoris with the gel, then gently pushed more lubricant inside me until I was moaning and grinding my hips.

'Let's take a ride,' he whispered and carried me over to the bench, mounting it behind me. We rode together, his fingers rolling my nipples whilst the tip of his cock nudged against my bottom, until I lifted myself off the saddle so he could enter me. His movements were long and slow until he began squeezing my breasts and I felt him quicken his pace to short, rapid jabs. Greedy again, I was rubbing myself against the leather pummel at the same time as he was penetrating me from behind and the total explosion as I dissolved into a million stars was phenomenal. He called out a name when he came but it wasn't mine and I was past caring. We are all entitled to our fantasies.

'Had you planned to stay the night?' he asked afterwards. Before I could answer he said, 'You're staying over.'

We heated Chinese food he'd brought in with him and drank more wine. Then I went to bed, leaving him watching the news. Very domestic. I drifted off to sleep before he came to bed and when I woke early next morning I was alone. I got dressed hurriedly in jeans and a sweater, feeling it would be less embarrassing to leave whilst he was out jogging or whatever.

But he appeared in the hallway just when I was about to let myself out and handed me a folded piece of paper. My notice to quit, I guessed. I was a bit fazed, wondering whether to be relieved or disappointed.

'Read it,' he said.

I unfolded the note. It simply gave his name and his mobile number. Underneath he'd written, 'Ring me for personal services.'

I looked up at him. 'Please ring me later,' he said. 'I want you to call me and make an appointment to come over again. Dress how you choose ... be as dominant as you like.'

He rang for a taxi and I rode home in some confusion. He could've had me again on a plate. Then it dawned on me that he was turned on by anticipation and that he'd been quite masterful with me, though I'd not felt threatened in any way. This could be fun.

But I didn't ring until about six that evening. He picked up the call on the second ring.

'Richard Cole,' was the terse response.

'This is Lady Tessa Delahaye,' I said in my best autocratic manner.

There was a sharp intake of breath. 'Yes, your ladyship,' he said.

'I should like a car to be sent round to collect me for my massage. I should warn you that I expect impeccable service.' I put the phone down. He knew my address. I didn't have very long to wait before there was a ring on the doorbell and I leaped to answer it. A driver and car awaited me and, after the short journey, I was back in the lift up to Mr C's apartment.

He answered the door straightaway. I strode into the hallway, ignoring him and stood, tapping my foot, waiting for him to help me off with my long black coat. I knew that I'd surprised him. Underneath, I wore my uniform: with the addition of thigh-length honey suede boots.

'Showtime, Mr Cole,' I said. I swung my tightly overalled bottom and headed for the master bedroom. He followed behind me. When I saw what was on the bed my mouth went dry. On top of the fur throw he'd placed a mask and a little crop. The riding bench stood close by. I was really playing with the grown-ups now.

'You're a dream come true,' he said huskily. 'You sound like a duchess, you look as if butter wouldn't melt in your mouth and you come on to me like a hooker.'

'For saying that, you need teaching a lesson,' I barked as I picked up the whip.

He moved over to the bench.

'Undress,' I said.

He obeyed. Then he clambered up and bent over the leather saddle. I found it quite difficult not to get too whip happy and wearing the mask and high boots was a turn-on but I must have judged things right because he cried out and asked me to give him a few more strokes before he'd let me finish.

When he stood facing me, I was tempted to kneel and cram his cock into my mouth but I insisted he finger-fuck me whilst I kept all my clothes on, including the mask. He had to squeeze his fingers inside my damp underwear to get at my pussy until I writhed, slippery under his hands, and he asked permission to take my uniform and knickers off.

'Then I want you to paint my pussy,' I commanded.

'Can I suck you first?'

'No,' I said.

Somehow we endured the delicious anticipation whilst he removed my clothing then we were on the bed and I reached for the items I'd left beside it. I was whimpering with anticipation as he parted my legs and began his task. The sable brush was much softer than even a female's finger, more deli-cate than even the gentlest of tongues. And, dipped in baby oil, the brush's caress was exquisite as it slid slowly back and forth in the hands of this master craftsman.

'You have a perfect pussy,' he murmured. 'It deserves to be painted.'

But I didn't answer. First, I wanted the brush to go faster. Then, I wanted it to slow down so I could beg for it. When he reached under me to stroke lubricant inside my tight little ring, my muscles tensed but the hussy that lives inside me turned me over onto my front for him. He had a vibrator at the ready and played it on me whilst I spread my legs, then got on to all fours so he could push deeper inside me. I heard myself groaning, gasping and telling him he could suck my pussy when he wanted to.

Gently, he withdrew the vibrator and turned me over. I closed my eyes as he knelt between my thighs and his lips and tongue explored me, devouring me, slurping and sucking my juices as if eating a mango. I was vowing to remember the name of the vanilla-flavoured stuff he used just as his lapping tongue found the right rhythm. 'Don't stop ... oh, don't stop,' I pleaded and, obeying my orders, he went on tonguing me until I was aching for release. I arched my back and soared.

He left me then and I went to run a shower. As I thought he would, he met me with a huge fluffy towel and then, wrapped in one of his bathrobes, I sat on the bed beside him.

He passed me the pot of vanilla gel and I realised he intended me to frig myself in front of him. With a flick of a remote control he brought up a movie for me to watch. A tiny blonde girl was tonguing and stroking a bigger black girl's nipples, which were standing out like loganberries against her ebony skin. Mr C caressed my nipples very gently with a vibrator, to and fro, whilst I watched the screen. When the black girl sucked on her fingers and reached into her blonde friend's pretty little bush, my fingers moved in time with hers. Watching the girls was making me pant with excitement.

Mr C was by then so aroused and I was so sticky that he pushed his penis inside me easily. I gasped as he drew my legs up over his shoulders so he was inside me right up to the hilt. His cock was moving in me slowly, deliberately, making me want it to go on and on forever but as his strokes quickened, I licked my own fingers and rippled them against my clitoris so that we finished together.

Later he talked a bit. It seemed he kept the apartment entirely separate from his home life and his wife used a hotel on the rare occasions she visited the city. I'd got him sussed. Then he told me that his PA had just given in her notice and that there was a job going, if I wanted it. The details would be emailed to the employment agency the next day. I told him I needed to think about it.

I didn't return to the apartment until the Tuesday when I knew he would be away. After spending several hours making sure everything was immaculate, I let myself out and took a cab to the agency offices.

Maz saw me straightaway. She looked sharply at me when I told her I wanted to quit.

'No funny business I hope,' she said.

'Nothing in the least funny,' I said.

'I'll let Mr Cole know,' she said. 'Have you got another job? Because, oddly enough, he's just contacted me, asking me to forward details of a PA job to our secretarial division. You could do it standing on your head.' She sounded reluctant.

'I can just imagine,' I said. 'But no, thank you. I can't handle that sort of commitment just now. I'll think about things for the time being.'

Maz gave me a long look whilst she tapped her teeth with a pencil. Then she shrugged and pushed my time sheet across the desk for the last time.

'I can only say, I hope you know what you're doing,' she said. 'I'm going to miss you.'

At six o'clock that evening, a courier arrived at my door. He delivered two-dozen yellow roses, a box of handmade chocolates and a note. The note said:

> I told you that you were wasting your skills
> by working as a cleaning operative. I can offer
> you a PA job with flexible hours to suit both of
> us with, possibly, some travel. And if you
> moved into my apartment, you could save on
> rent. This is a strings-free offer though I can't
> promise there won't be a few stings.

Thanking Vesuvius
Primula Bond

The idea of swinging in a hammock above the Bay of Naples seemed like utter heaven when Samantha first suggested it. We were sitting in the British Museum at the time, staring at the shrivelled remains of someone who had failed to escape the eruption of Mount Vesuvius in AD 79. Every six months or so we'd meet there for some sisterly bonding, to ponder the exhibits until we felt sufficiently educated. Then we'd repair to the pub so that we could catch up – or rather I could listen to tales of her doomed love life.

'Except that I don't really have a love life at the moment, unlike you, lucky thing.' Samantha sighed, tapping my engagement ring as we waited to cross the road. 'How is the mysterious Geoffrey, by the way?'

I conjured up my imaginary fiancé from the collage of magazine cuttings stuck to my pin board at home. I love my younger sister, but she's too nosy by half. I had to invent Geoffrey to keep her and my other friends off my back.

'He's fine. In the States, actually. Dying to meet you.'

'Which is why you'd be the ideal travelling companion. Respectable, spoken for, always available ...

There's an extra space in the villa, you see. You love the sun, or you used to. You're a brilliant cook. There'll be plenty of culture. And you won't be competition when we're out pulling the locals.'

'We?' I paused at the door of the pub.

'Me and Greta. Don't look so horrified.' Sam flicked her golden plaits at me. 'She speaks English really well now. We're best mates.' Now she was blushing.

'For some reason clients always want us on modelling assignments together.'

'You mean you still haven't twigged why identical *Frauleins* in scraps of lace and shaking their booties like the Cheeky Girls is such a winner?' I said, with not a little trace of incredulity at her naivety. It was then I caught sight of my dishevelled reflection in the tarnished pub mirror – long hair falling out of a chaotic top knot, big eyes watering over the emerald-green pashmina protecting my face from the late spring chill. I was not so much cheeky as peaky.

'I suppose we *are* alike –'

'You're their best investment since what's her name, who's always in the society pages. Come on, doll. Why do the pair of you want someone like me coming on your girlie holiday?'

'We don't, really.' Sam bit her lip and pushed her way to the bar to order my favourite Merlot.

'Oh, that's charming.'

'I mean, it's the agency who suggested it. In fact they'll only let us have the time off if we take a kind of –'

'What? Minder?'

Sam giggled. Even her laugh made me feel

ungainly and ancient, but protective too. I'd looked after her since our mum died, done everything for her until the talent scouts took over and it was time for me to get a life.

'Chaperone. Apparently we're not considered proper adults, even at the age of twenty. They don't want us misbehaving and ruining our looks for the Gleneagles shoot next month.' She pouted her pillowy mouth. 'You're even to make sure we don't get sunburned.'

The idea of swinging in a hammock over the Bay of Naples with a pair of nubile honeys in tow would not have been my first suggestion for an ideal holiday – but it didn't stop me from accepting the offer. I even wangled for the holiday to be paid through the agency and, after some toing and froing, cast caution to the chill wind and went for it.

The peachy villa was paradise regained. Hidden in a lush garden on top of a pink cliff overlooking a small, deserted beach, it had cool flagstoned floors with terracotta tubs of huge cacti dotted about the poolside terrace and entrance. Tiny finches darted about the bougainvillea and the whole place hummed with life and heat. And right there was the hammock I'd imagined, slung especially for me between two black pine trees.

The days passed without incident. I relaxed on the terrace while the girls gossiped about the agency and the high dramas that seemed to occur with regularity in that world of fragile egos and beautiful creatures. I read the latest blockbuster novels, dozed in the shade and took photos of the landscape.

We were near the end of our week's sojourn when my girls got restless – as young girls do. I was on the terrace, as usual, dunking almond biscuits into my cappuccino while they sipped at pressed lemon juice. As always, I had flung a kaftan over my bathing suit before joining them for breakfast but, as soon as I got outside, the heat sucked at me. I paced about on the hot stones, desperate to take it off, take everything off, and jump into the pool.

'Carla says it's a heatwave,' murmured Sam, fanning herself with my newspaper. 'And that's some achievement in a place that regularly reaches thirty degrees. If you look towards the mainland, you can see smoke from the forest fires.'

Carla was round the corner of the house, dressed in her smart white maid's uniform. We watched her snapping out sheets to hang on the line. No wet patches under her long brown arms. The heatwave evidently didn't bother her.

'We're safer here, then,' I said, 'unless we take that trip to Pompeii.'

Sam and Greta shook their heads. They were extraordinary. Even their jerky, haughty movements were the same. They had cut their hair before coming on holiday, long white-blonde fringes swept sideways across their narrow faces, but cropped close at the back so that their exposed necks were raw, like stalks.

'We'll suffocate if we stay here. But, please, not Pompeii. Not today.' Greta stood up, twitching a shiny triangle of pink thong across her waxed pubes. I didn't know where to look, because she was topless too, her small round breasts jutting on her ribcage, daring me to stare.

'Bone,' I said.

Greta squinted through the shadows cast by the vine above her head.

'It's all I can see of you, sweetie ... skin and bone.'

'We want to go down to the beach,' they said.

I swerved away from her and spilled coffee all over my kaftan.

'Whatever,' I sighed. 'Let the agency treat you like cut glass china. You can do what you like.'

I stepped on to the parched grass area and into the sun. I could hear Carla singing in the sizzling air. My hair seemed to be frying on my scalp and my blood drummed in my ears as my body struggled to adjust to the attack of temperature. Sweat dribbled between my breasts, but I liked it. I liked the way the ferocious heat seemed to coax them into fullness, pushing against the material of the kaftan, the heat spreading all over my skin. Already there were little freckles on my arms. I'd been skulking in the hammock most of the time, except when the girls went inside to chatter to Carla, or have a siesta, and that was when I dived into the pool before lying out on the stones beside it like a slowly roasting lizard, alone with my big white body. But right now I was too shy and self-conscious to bare myself in front of anyone.

The pool was calling to me, but I wouldn't fully uncover myself in front of them.

'Take that kaftan off,' said Sam. 'It's absurd to have that on in this heat.'

'I shouldn't,' I said. 'I'm not like you two – all slender and perfect. There's far too much of me.'

'That's so not true.' Greta opened a raffia bag and

started pulling out jewel-bright, diaphanous sarongs, as if she were a magician. 'You are beautiful, Laura. You're all woman. One day I will give all this up and eat chocolate so I can look like you again.'

Sam snorted and sat up. 'But I daresay your Geoffrey likes a nice big handful, eh, sis? Come on, don't be shy. Show us! It's the hottest summer they've seen for decades, and you're all covered up in your old kaftan.'

She and Greta danced around me like marionettes, spindly arms and fingers teasing me, enormous blue eyes flashing above their sharp cheekbones, and then the kaftan was off, flung across the grass.

'Now you're ready for the beach. Won't you try a bikini?' Sam surveyed me, hands on her hips. At least she still had her top on. 'I think you'd look rather splendid, and there are lovely little shops in the town.'

'Don't push it,' I warned, crossing my arms uselessly over my stomach. 'I don't want to scare the natives.'

'The natives! Now you're talking. What are we doing hiding up here like a trio of nuns?' Sam shoved her sunglasses on and started packing up her beach bag. 'Sun. Sea. Sex. Bring it on!'

'Let me tie this sarong for you.' Greta was beside me, pushing my hands away. She reached round me to wrap a length of smoky blue chiffon round my hips, rubbing like a cat against me. When she moved back her dark-red nipples were huge and prominent.

'You were almost the same shape as me, Sammy,

before you dieted yourself into oblivion,' I chattered nervously over Greta's shoulder.

'You can't have big tits and child-bearing hips on the catwalk, Laura,' mocked Sam, snatching up the keys to the hired jeep and stalking into the house. 'Even if you have got better legs than me.'

'Fantastic legs. But you shouldn't hide the tits and hips, either,' murmured Greta, bending to pick up her bikini top. She faced me, smiling at my relief as she tied it over those astounding nipples. 'Someone will want to enjoy those.'

Out of the corner of my eye I saw Carla pick my kaftan off the grass and hold it to her face as she watched us go.

There was no shade on the beach, apart from the thatched deck of a little bar at the far end. The air seemed to be solid in the soupy heat, but there was the tiniest breeze coming off the dazzling water. I followed the girls down the rocky slope, laden with towels and mats and bottles and books.

'Where are you going to lie?' I asked anxiously. 'You've got to watch the sun.'

The cove was idyllic, quiet, almost deserted apart from a scattering of sun worshippers. A couple of surfer dudes were wading out of the sea looking like Greek gods. Or Roman gods, I suppose, as we were in Ischia. One of these sons of Poseidon wore a wetsuit rolled down over a ridged brown torso and carried a diver's tank. The other had on a pair of faded denim shorts and his skin was the colour of golden syrup. He shook his bleached hair off his face like a dog. The water made runnels through the dark hair on their stomachs and down their strong thighs.

Sam nudged Greta and they went into catwalk mode, swinging hips and ankles athletically across the sand, kicking at the water and tilting their chins over their shoulders as they passed. The boys gaped, as any red-blooded male would do, and muttered some kind of greeting.

I realised I'd stopped on the edge of the sand. My tongue was running across my dry lips as I watched the boys watching the girls. My imaginary Geoffrey had a new face now, modelled on those gods, and a new body to match. Those young buttocks, flexing – it was amazing. Those thighs, swaggering like a cowboy's, as if his dick swung too low. Those brown hands, slapping at each other's shoulders as they parted.

The guy in the shorts walked across the beach. Greta and Sam had chosen a spot and were waggling their hands at me. He nodded as he passed them. After shaking his longish hair off his face again, he went up to the bar and unlocked the door.

'Laura! We need the sun cream!' the girls yelled.

The other guy, the diver, had nearly reached me. I hitched my cargo of beach stuff awkwardly in my arms. He was right in front of me, scuffing through the sand, and I tipped my head towards the girls.

'Demanding little madams,' I said, smiling straight at him. 'Gorgeous, though, aren't they?'

He shrugged. Obviously he hadn't understood. He bent to pick up a magazine that I'd dropped and glanced at the model on the cover. The eyelashes fringing his amber eyes were stuck together with salt water, and drops were gathered along his collar bone. He handed me the magazine, but I couldn't take my eyes off his mouth. He had obscenely full lips, like his mate. The kind of lips you could imagine kissing, then nibbling down your neck, over your breasts, sucking on your taut nipples, kissing your stomach, pushing down, down . . .

'I didn't notice,' he said suddenly, brushing past me to walk up the slope. I could smell his sweat mixed with the hot rubber of his wetsuit. His voice was low, the voice of a much older man, and with an almost perfect English accent.

I let out a kind of shivering laugh of denial, and bustled off towards the girls.

The blond guy started up some music, and the few other people on the beach raised their heads testily.

'Remember your duties,' said Sam, snatching the sun cream off me and kneeling up behind Greta, who had taken her top off again and was staring out to sea. 'Got to keep the sun off.'

'I think it's too hot already,' murmured Greta, closing her eyes. Sam smoothed the cream on to Greta's back with exaggerated movements, nuzzling into her neck and letting her hands trail round to her breasts and stomach. She glanced across the beach. Sure enough the barman was leaning on his counter, tipping beer into his mouth, and I swear he was massaging the front of his shorts.

His diver mate had reached the top of the slope. My stomach lurched as he hoisted up a surfboard, muscles flexing down his sides. Come down, come back down here. He stared at Greta and Sam, then propped the surfboard against his jeep and started to peel his wetsuit over his hips. A line of hair ran down his stomach, leading into his groin. I ached to see what was there; the proud thing he no doubt possessed quivering out of his wetsuit. I breathed quickly, impatiently. It was safe to look. He'd never imagine I was lusting after him. I was invisible beside the dazzling young girls; a motherly figure in my sarong and my big straw hat.

'Come on, Laura. Your turn.' Greta knocked me to my knees and whipped my hat off. My hair tumbled down, warm coils on my skin. Sam giggled, dancing round us while she undid her top. Greta pushed me on to my front and Sam stole my sarong, running into the sea with it trailing behind her like a wing.

'When did you last have a man inside you?' Greta whispered, sitting astride me and dripping oil on to my spine. 'I see you looking, Laura. You look at everyone.'

I tried to push her off me. I wanted to see the diver naked, but she locked me between her thighs and rocked her neat butt over mine as she pulled my bathing suit down to my waist and stroked the oil up and down so that my skin started tingling in places she hadn't even reached. My thighs were squeezed together and the lips of my pussy were stuck with moisture.

'The last time I was on a beach, actually, a few years ago,' I groaned as her fingertips dug into me. The jeep's rackety engine fired up. So he was leaving. 'I was cute then, like you. Slim, sex on legs, tits that stayed put when I moved.'

'So you looked just like Sam?' Greta flicked my hair off my shoulder and massaged my neck. 'But you're still sexy now. You still have these amazing breasts – so big, so juicy.' I blushed into the towel and let loose with some information that I thought would either shock or amuse young Greta.

'My boyfriend had the biggest dick you've ever seen. Constantly bursting out of his Speedos, he was.' My pussy twitched at the memory. I was definitely wet down there. 'Oh, the heat. It made us so horny.'

'It was Geoffrey?' she asked.

'Oh no. Long before his time. But that's how it was back then. We were always at it, especially on holiday. Grabbed at sex like we were starving.'

Just then Sam called out and Greta slipped off me. Sam was dancing about coquettishly as the barman shook cocktails. Greta went over to them and snaked an arm around Sam's waist.

On the other side of the beach the diver had left his surfboard and wetsuit by the rocks, but his jeep was roaring up the dusty track, scattering stones. I crawled over the hot sand to where Sam had dropped my sarong. Hell, no one was looking. I stood up and stretched. The light danced off the water. I couldn't resist. I flung myself in and washed all that heat and sweat off me until all I could hear was my own heart drumming.

And later, while my girls nibbled shellfish at the bar, I lay down and let the sun sink into me while I dozed off. A young cock remembered, hot and swollen from hours in the sun, nudging between my loose, lazy thighs, waking me, pushing up inside where I was always so ready, now so empty, invading all that moist darkness with solid inches of pumping, thrusting, thrusting . . .

'How can you bear it out here? You're not even burned. We've been in the shade all day.'

Their shadows were blocking out the still blazing afternoon sun.

'Must be my natural habitat.' I yawned, sitting up. Only the stiffening of my nipples told me that my bathing suit had slipped down. I pulled it up slowly and reluctantly, relishing the kiss of the sun on my breasts.

Both girls had hands on hips in slightly defensive gestures.

'We don't want to go yet,' Sam said, as I moved in slow motion to gather our things. 'Paulo's mate is coming back soon, and we're going to party.'

I couldn't focus. They jumped like stick insects against the glare of sun. My head was thick with sleep and the sweaty dreams of summer sex I'd been drowning in.

'Whatever. But just remember, it's only a couple of days before I hand you back.' I rubbed my eyes. 'They'll roast me alive if you misbehave.'

'So stay with us,' said Greta, rearranging my shoulder straps. 'Have some fun.'

'Oh, honey. I'd cramp your style.'

The other guy's jeep was skidding up in a cloud of dust, eager to get the party started. I made my excuses, and headed instead towards the track and turned to wave. Greta was watching me go while Sam tugged at her. The boy in the hut was nodding his head to some music and rolling a joint. And, above the dust cloud, out over the sea, still that wispy trail of smoke from the forest fires.

'You're going home now?'

The diver was dry now, his hair glossy and black, and he was wearing a ripped black T-shirt. I could see the pulse going in his neck. I realised that the erotic dreams I'd been having on the beach came with this face attached, this body. Hidden under my sarong, I ached for him.

He seemed to be waiting for me to answer, but I was so warm, so weak with imagined pleasure that all I could do was smile weakly at him, shrug casually as if sad to miss the fun, and move on past.

Early next morning it was hotter than ever. I was up, dressed and eager to go. After breakfast there was still no sign of the girls, so I stamped up to Sam's room.

Carla came out, delicately wiping her upper lip. 'They are sick, *signora*,' she said. 'They ate bad fish at the beach.'

She looked flushed, and two buttons of her white uniform were undone to reveal the deep crack of her cleavage.

'Hung-over, more like,' I said. 'Now we'll all be in trouble, and it's almost the last day.' I flung open the door. 'We're going to Pompeii. It'll take a whole day to get there and back.'

Their shuttered bedroom was like a perfumed oven. The villa had several bedrooms, but they'd chosen to share – no doubt sharing the secrets and giggling over the things that amuse young women of their age. The ceiling fan flicked round, stirring expensive musky aromas around the room.

'We can't go,' Sam groaned.

The shutters clattered open. Greta was in Sam's

bed, one arm flung across my sister's body and apparently fast asleep.

'Did you stay at the beach too late last night?' I demanded, staying by the window. 'What did you get up to in that shack? And why is Greta in your bed?'

'What are you, my mother?'

Greta lifted her hand to hush Sam's mouth.

My breath was difficult to catch. 'That's what I'm here for, isn't it? To keep an eye on you?'

Sam shakily wiped her forehead. Her hair was drenched with sweat. 'They weren't interested. We had fun, but those blokes are weird. They didn't want to fuck us. They were probably too stoned.'

Greta opened her blue eyes and grinned across at me. 'Perhaps they didn't like me kissing Sam with my tongue. Some men get a hard-on to see that, but –'

'Shut up, Greta, you'll upset her,' growled Sam. 'Laura's not into all that.'

'I'm going to Pompeii,' I snapped. 'I think you should come.'

'You won't rest till you've had your fix of culture, will you?' Sam pouted petulantly and then sank back on to the pillow.

Greta looked at me. 'She is sick, you know, Laura. You go get your fix alone.'

That Oscar Wilde was right. Youth is so wasted on the young.

The coach growled and swayed around the winding coast road. Here on the mainland the sky was smudged grey with smoke from the forest fires. I glanced across the bay to Ischia, where my girls lay nursing their headaches in their stifling room above the deserted beach. My insides tightened as I imagined Greta fondling Sam, straddling her as the sheet slipped off, leaning forwards to kiss her with her tongue.

I wanted to keep watch, to throw a bucket of cold water over them. But I also felt liberated, alone in this air-conditioned coach, away for a few hours from their knowing perfection. The only other people who could stand the heat were an elderly couple and a scruffy group of students.

Pompeii was everything I'd expected. The sizzling, deadly heat was just right to create the doomed atmosphere, as was the noonday sky darkened with the threat of fire. I trailed through the ruined shops and houses, past columns with no roof to support, along the narrow streets where chariots used to race, flapping my guidebook in front of me and wrapping my shoulders with yet another sarong. The heat scrambled my brain. I gave up trying to concentrate on the details and just absorbed the history.

'And this was a bordello,' said the deep voice of a tour guide behind me as I wandered into a warren of tiny chambers. 'These were the whores' rooms. Those shelves were the beds where they pleasured their clients.'

My blood buzzed in my ears. I'd imagined the voice. Sex dominated my mind completely. I blamed the heat. I was being stupid, trying to feel twenty again. I couldn't get Sam and Greta out of my mind. I couldn't stop the ache that had begun yesterday when I yearned to see the diver's emerging young body, made worse by Greta oiling me in the sun and asking me when I last had a man . . .

The other sightseers were trailing back to the coach. I leaned against the wall, limp with frustration, and closed my eyes.

'The blonde lady from the beach.'

Then came the smell of sweat and of man, mixed not with rubber this time but fresh laundry. A white shirt sleeve blocked my way out. The sunlight was extinguished, but the heat inside my belly was even greater.

'The diver from the beach,' I gasped aloud, wetting my lips. My body seemed to be licked by fire. 'What are you doing here?'

'I'm a part-time tourist guide. It's my job, among other things.' He laughed, framing me with his other arm. Close up, and fully clothed, he looked older – in his 40s, I'd say; one of those guys who has spent a lifetime outdoors being rangy and rugged. He was close up against me now, the buckle of his trousers jabbing through my flimsy dress. His legs trapped me against the old wall. 'So where are your frisky little bodyguards? Left you alone for once?'

'It's the other way round, actually. I'm supposed to be looking after *them*.' I wanted to kick myself, sounding so prim. 'So . . . I don't know what you did to them at the beach last night, but –'

'I didn't do anything to them,' he said, sounding shocked. He shook his head, his eyes gleaming. I could feel the long hard shape of his cock through his trousers pressing up against me, and a shaft of excitement shot up the back of my legs.

'It's you I'd like to have sex with.'

I shook my head so hard it banged against the rough wall, breathy laughter sputtering out of my mouth. I was imagining things, surely, although the thrust of that cock was real all right. I could definitely feel it trying to nuzzle through my skirt, into my bush. I tried to sidle sideways, but my legs wouldn't hold me up.

'So little room in here, don't you think?' I blustered nervously. 'I thought I was in a bakery. Or is it a police station? What are these cells? What did you say this place was?' I slithered along the wall, craning my head this way and that. I was seeing nothing, so aware of his body right up against me, all that maleness pulsing into the cooked air.

'It was called the *lupanare*. The frescoes should give you a clue. Take a good look.'

He pulled me away from the wall and, balancing one hand on my hip, fingers feeling my flesh, he pointed upwards. Very faint, cracked figures, painted in terracotta and black, were etched over the ancient bricks. At first I thought they were dancing, or praying, but no. They were copulating, rutting, humping, in every position under the sun. Here was a tough man gripping a slender girl's thighs while she stretched out gracefully and he fucked her from behind. There was a woman with elegant coiled hair straddling a man's cock as he reclined on cushions.

'It's like a menu, see? All the services you could get for your *dinarii*.' He whispered right into my ear. 'Or perhaps the pictures were just the porno of the day – pictures designed to get them horny.'

There was such a heavy silence in the chamber that I felt as if I were being sucked right into the frescoes. Another pair knelt up and went at it face to face, togas slipping to the floor. A man simply stood, displaying his thumping erection. A woman solemnly lowered her face into a man's groin. Another woman sat on the bed with them, staring directly at me.

'Do you think they were still in here when the lava came?' I was leaning against him now. The etchings were so delicate, yet so businesslike. Imagine giving pleasure for money. God, I could be there, selling myself, climbing on to a great meaty penis and lowering myself down, down on to its rigid shaft...

'Were they petrified exactly as it found them, you know, *in flagrante*?'

'Some of them, yes. But what a way to go.' Now both his hands were resting on my hips. I was too turned on to resist as he started to tug my silky dress up my legs. 'Imagine coming to visit your favourite tart after a long day's hard work, paying your fee, fucking her senseless or getting her to suck you off, getting all tangled up and hot on the bed, with not a clue what's happening to the city outside these walls; just lost inside her, pumping your life away.'

He ran his fingers up under my dress and sank them into the soft flesh of my buttocks, lifting me quickly so that I was forced to wrap my legs round him. The sarong slipped off my shoulders and landed on his foot. I could feel my sex lips slicking open, moistening in the lacy knickers as my dress floated round my waist. Now his eyes were on a level with my breasts and we both looked down at them, bulging honey-dark in the half-light.

There were still people about. Footsteps scraping along in the dust outside.

'They wouldn't have stopped, would they, even if their hearts were clattering with fear?' I said, throwing back my head and arching my throat as my nipples hardened against the tight bodice of my dress. 'They would have gone on and on, saying, "Don't stop until I come; whatever it is can't touch us in here."'

The diver carried me round the corner out of sight and slammed me against the wall.

'That's right. Safe inside the *lupanare*. Everyone fucking like there's no tomorrow.'

He dug his fingers into my butt cheeks, easing them apart, and then his fingers were in the damp crack between them, searching and sliding over my tender flesh. I couldn't tell whether it was sweat or whether I was creaming myself, waiting for the moment. I was alive with excitement now, opening myself wider to swallow his fingers, to grip him, grinding myself against his white shirt, staining it with my juices as I wound my fingers in his hair to smother him between my damp breasts.

He groaned unevenly as his fingers slid in and out of me, releasing my urgent, musky scent, driving me wild with wanting. I slid my hand down his stomach to find it, scrabbled at his belt, grinning at the bestial grunting noises I was making as his teeth easily tore my flimsy dress and nipped sharply at the nipple sparking there.

Suddenly there were soft, questioning voices jostling in the doorway, coming in, coming round the corner, the click of a camera, and then a gasp. A stifled giggle, then another gasp and another click of the camera before the feet shuffled away.

He lifted his head, lips wet with his saliva, and we stared at each other, eyes glittering in the suffocating gloom. I was quivering violently now, with the effort of gripping him and with the ferocious desire to have him, right there in our own hot whore house.

'So now they have all seen us.' He swore under his breath, his face so close to mine. 'I have to go. I have to join my group.'

'Fuck your group,' I snapped. 'Let them come and see. Let's recreate the energy of the old bordello.' I kissed him hard, pressing my mouth on to his gorgeous lips. He paused, then his tongue snaked hungrily around mine and I let my feet drop to the floor and we staggered backwards into one of the little alcoves which used to be the sumptuous couches of lust.

I barely felt the scratch of rough stone against my back as we fell and he reared over me on his hands and knees, just like one of the hungry men in the etchings. I unzipped his trousers and there was his big penis standing hard and straight and there were my legs, hooking him into me.

He edged across the narrow shelf. How tiny those Pompeiians must have been! I was half raised against the wall, but our bodies were stuck together now and there was the round tip of his cock opening me up, then the long, smooth shaft sliding in. I was so wet now, so smooth compared with the rough stone of our makeshift bed. My arms and legs were wound around him and his hands were squeezing my breasts, pinching my nipples as he bit my neck, pausing to listen for any audience, and then we were rocking wildly together, his cock thrusting and bursting and filling me totally.

Outside there were more voices and some shouting and laughter, but they receded, and then one or two coaches sounded their horns. I laughed, and threw myself back against the stone bed. His full weight was on me, shoving me up against the wall as he did what was natural. His knees were scratched, my shoulder blades were scratched, but then what sounded like some kind of siren wailed up in the city of Naples and a helicopter whirred overhead. My diver started to groan again, and I thought of where we were – the volcano and all its eruptions gathering over us. I laughed to myself as I felt my own underground currents drawing and pulling, gathering into a point, sucking me under, sucking him in, and the commotion outside and the prospect of crowds of tourists pouring in to see the show only drove my excitement on until I felt him shudder. I was too excited to hold back and, grinding myself against him, I came too, wave after wave of glorious ecstasy rippling in and out of both of us until we could catch our breath again.

I could barely walk as we staggered out of the *lupanare* and back through the ruined town to the car park.

'The fires are all along the coast now,' said my diver as we got to my coach. He wrapped my sarong around my neck, fingers lingering on my skin. 'If we don't go now we'll all be trapped.'

The sky was a venomous yellow and there was a scorching and ripping in the air.

'Somehow that doesn't scare me,' I said. 'I'd like to be trapped here with you.'

'I'll meet you on the beach tonight,' he called as he backed towards his own bus. 'If Geoffrey doesn't mind.'

He was pointing at my finger. The girls must have told him I was spoken for, though that hadn't stopped him seducing me in the *lupanare*, had it? I took the false engagement ring off, held it up so that it glinted against the livid sky, then threw it over the wall to be buried in the dust of Pompeii.

'It's a date.' I laughed. As my bus rumbled back towards the coast, I looked up at Mount Vesuvius – and thanked her for the favour she had done me.

Primula Bond is the author of the Black Lace novels *Club Crème* and *Country Pleasures*, as well as the Nexus novel *Behind the Curtain*.

A Dirty Job Melissa Harrison

When her boss finally pushes into her, it's so deep that she gasps, an involuntary flinch making her pull away for an instant before his grip on her right hip tightens through her indecently short skirt and she arches back into the rhythm of his stroke. Her face is pressed hard into the glassy shine of his deep mahogany desk, her unseeing eyes fixed on the vast river-view his huge corner office affords over the sparkling bend of the river. The desk is cold on her breasts, her nipples hard where her unbuttoned blouse has exposed them; her full weight rests on her chest, as with his left hand he holds both her wrists pinned high behind her back.

He pulls out (the loss of him inside her sudden, shocking) and moves his right hand up slightly to the small of her back, finding the dimple above her buttock and he places his thumb into it, gently, possessively, almost meditatively. Kate can still feel the head of his cock, wet with her, nudging gently at her pussy, which aches for him again. She feels his foot kick her legs even further apart; not gently, but dispassionately. She does what he wants, teetering slightly in her heels, making herself even more available to him, and he drives back into her again, hard, his resumption a reward for her acquiescence. Each stroke ends in a bruising thud as he fills her up; it's almost painful, but deeply satisfying nevertheless. She longs not so much to come, but to feel him come inside her.

The seat covering is hot and scratchy against Kate's face as she rouses herself from her fantasy, the lilting rhythm of the train having conspired to lull her into a dreamy half-sleep. Squinting against the dying rays of a glorious winter sunset, she sees the evening light catch the windows of the tall office block where she works, winking at her from across the water as the train carries her away. She finds herself shockingly aroused, here amongst dozens of closely packed strangers, and feels a guilty flush rise from her neck to her face as if the images she has involuntarily summoned are somehow visible to her fellow-passengers. Looking down at her lap, she lets the fantasy go, knowing how impossible it is; Mr Stevens may technically be one of her bosses, and only a couple of years older than her at that, but as a part-time cleaner at the huge insurance firm she is under no illusions that he would even know her name.

The next day Kate's eyes are fixed on the office block again as it swings back into view around the bend in the river. She times her arrival to coincide with the main flurry of departures at the end of the day; unlike the rest of the six-strong cleaning team, who come from jobs at other buildings, the company is her only employer. During the day she works in a clothes shop, part of a big chain selling overpriced fashion to dead-eyed teenagers with too much money and no sense.

Though she's still slim, Kate's body is made imperfect, in her eyes, by stretch marks. She can still

fit into the strappy vests and hipster shorts she
spends the day sorting and folding and, at 26, she's
certainly not too old; but Kate feels a world away
from wanting to show off her body in that way.
She's tired a lot of the time, and has got into the
habit of avoiding mirrors, though, when she does
catch sight of herself, what she sees isn't what the
men who pass her slowly on the street see, looking
back over their shoulders, or, like here on the train,
surreptitiously glancing over at her. There is a raw
sensuality to her every movement that marks her
out as a woman, not a girl, and which shines out –
to everyone but her.

At the office Kate pushes her way through the
smart, be-suited crowd surging out through the
revolving door, working her way slowly against the
flow. They are putting on their coats as they leave,
making calls on their mobiles; in black, dun and
grey they barely register her, flowing around her
like a pebble in a stream. She swipes her card at the
turnstile, smiling at the guards who are just chang-
ing shift. They smile back, two pairs of eyes following her as she hurries to the lift. They like her; she
knows their names – on top of which, she moves
with an easy grace that is somehow different from
the tailored office girls that stream past them, none
of whom ever look over. Even the secretaries with
their short skirts and blusher, their hair uniformly
straightened, their acrylic nails defiantly impracti-
cal; even they have nothing on Kate.

A couple of hours later and she's nearly finished
the floor she's been allocated this week; disappoint-
ingly, it's not the one that houses Mr Stevens's office
(secretly she thinks of him as Adam, the name on

his desk), but the next one up. This floor contains meeting rooms and conference facilities; it doesn't need much in the way of cleaning, as a rule; just the bins emptied, the hoover run around and the desks and tables wiped down.

Dragging the squat, red vacuum cleaner with its incongruously smiling face by its electrical flex (in contravention of all the safety instructions), Kate begins   to make her way into the boardroom, backwards, the heavy door silent in the deep pile of the carpet, a J-cloth and trigger spray in her other hand. There's a few bars of a song going around in her head; she's not sure what; it's been stuck there all day. But turning into the room, the door still only ajar, she sees something that drives it out of her mind for good.

To one side of the polished expanse of the huge mahogany table, Mr Stevens is moving gently, his eyes closed, his chest bare. There is a moment when Kate's brain struggles to keep up; wonders not why his shirt is off, but only what he's doing in the boardroom so late at night. But a second later and, with a rush of blood to her face, she understands. And in another second, she understands yet more: though the face is turned away from her, the feet she can see under the table, in front of his, are still shackled by the unmistakeable folds of a pair of men's overalls. Mr Stevens is fucking a man.

Kate doesn't move; despite her shock, she's transfixed by the concentration on his face, as well as by the breadth of his shoulders and the pleasing shape of his torso, which she can see tapers to a nicely trim waist. She had imagined his chest to be smooth, for some reason; in reality he's neatly hairy, with the hair converging into a dark line which points down his flat stomach to where it is obscured by the round buttocks he now grips with such concentration. As she watches, he pulls slowly out; she can see the length of his cock, rigid and swollen, for a second only before he plunges it back into the other man's body.

Instantly she feels that she's wet, her pussy aching, an irresistible pulse starting up deep inside her; her heart pounds as she watches his slow movements of a moment before become fast and urgent. A few thrusts later, each one deeper and more merciless than the last, and he pulls out again; but this time he takes his straining cock in his hand and, in a second's work, shoots spurt after spurt of come onto the flushed buttocks before him. Still looking down, he smears it, full-palm, over the other man's skin, his thumb disappearing briefly and exploratively into the crevice of his ass; only then does Mr Stevens break his trance and look up, his eyes instantly meeting Kate's and locking on to hers where she stands only partially concealed by the door, the three of them making a bizarre, yet highly charged tableaux. And in that moment, despite her surprising arousal and overwhelming embarrassment, something passes between Kate and her boss; something she doesn't yet understand.

The bath is hot and deep and Kate sinks back into it gratefully. She's exhausted. She imagines what a luxury it would be to have someone run her bath, cook for her, look after her and put her to bed. But that person doesn't exist, so the next best thing is to do it herself. So now, here she is, her hair pinned up, her body hidden beneath mounds of bubbles, a cold beer balanced on the edge of the bath.

As if waiting for just this opportunity, the image of Adam fucking the unidentified man sidles inexorably into her head. Can he really be gay? She can see so clearly his look of total and utter concentration, the sheer sensuousness of his movements. Although still attended by a flush of something – maybe guilt – at having caught him in so intimate an act, Kate finds no revulsion or distaste at what he was doing; in fact, as she examines her response now, with the benefit of a few hours' grace, she finds her attraction to him remains undiminished. How strange; watching men fuck is not something she's ever fantasised about before. Could it be that she'd never really considered Mr Stevens available in the first place? Or is it just that it's fucking she loves and misses so much – fucking of any kind?

Now Kate's hand trails down through the water to gently explore herself; just thinking about sex has made her pussy swell and she can feel that telltale warmth curling through her. She takes a swig of beer, then dangles the bottle onto the floor and hooks one leg up over the side of the bath, the better to touch the soft folds of her sex where it blossoms under the warm water. In no hurry, she circles her clit where it is starting to harden, her eyes closing, her mind clearing of everything but the sensation she is producing. Slipping a finger inside, she feels the smoothness of her cunt, here at the centre, and suddenly remembers how she used to love to keep it all this smooth; how sensuous it was, how naked. Why did she stop shaving, and when? She can hardly remember. But now, as turned on as she is, she wants to be clean-shaven again.

She stands up, letting the soapy water ooze down her body, and reaches for a small mirror and the razor and gel she keeps for her legs. She sits on the side of the bath, spreads her legs and positions the mirror on the opposite edge so she can clearly see the pinkly engorged lips and the downy hair. Gently massaging the shaving gel around her cunt to form a lather, she feels an actual ache start up inside, she's that aroused; but she takes the razor and, with firm and definite strokes, shaves her entire pussy smooth and pink and clean.

Splashing water on to it from the bath makes her realise how much more sensitive it is like this; her clit in particular feels sensitised, as well as oddly vulnerable. She pauses before removing the mirror, choosing instead to leave it there and stay sitting on the side of the bath, where she can watch her fingers as they play with her newly denuded pussy. Pushing one finger, then two, inside, they emerge slick with her juices; she can see them glisten as she brings the moisture up to coat her swollen clit. She keeps her legs spread wide, liking what she sees, as the sudden vision of Adam's cock, rigid in his hand, shooting spurt after spurt of come tips her over the edge into a bucking, dizzying orgasm.

'So he's not gay?' Kate fails to keep the surprise out of her voice. 'I mean, I suppose I'd just assumed . . .'

'Adam?' Crystal, her supervisor, laughs richly. 'No, he's not gay. He's fucked every secretary who's worked here, love, and a few more. I'm surprised he's not had a go at you'.

Confused, Kate turns around, busies herself in the store cupboard. It's the next night and she's arrived for her shift a little early, hoping, uncharacteristically, to have time to talk to the others first, see what she can turn up. It's proved to be much easier than she'd expected.

'Why are you asking, anyway?' Crystal narrows her black eyes at her 'What have you heard, girl? Or are you carrying a torch?'

Before the blush rises and gives Kate away, Crystal is distracted by a crash, followed by curses, in the corridor. Going to investigate, with Kate at her heels, they find one of the building's many maintenance man sprawled on the carpet, his ankles tangled in a metal bucket, floored by a mop handle. Though his blue overalls give Kate a jolt of recognition, she wouldn't have been sure if, looking up, he hadn't blushed to the roots of his blond hair.

Scrambling up, apologising, his eyes never leave hers. 'Well, I've got to get on, love,' says Crystal, glancing, amused, at the two of them. She winks broadly at Kate before picking up the mop and bucket and making her way slowly down the corridor. Kate suddenly finds herself looking at her shoes. Must get changed, she thinks. Can't clean in heels.

There is a long silence.

'The other night,' he begins, 'I saw you leave. I know you probably think – I mean, it must seem to you like – and I'm not – I mean, Adam's not. He's not – you know. I've never done that before. He just –'

Here he stops, discomfited, his shoes suddenly

holding great allure for him too. Kate wonders why he's telling her at all.

'It's none of my business,' she begins. 'I don't even know him. I've never spoken to him. I just come in and clean. I'm not going to say anything to anyone, you know.' She looks down again, smoothes her skirt.

'No, I know, I just – it's not that; it's just that I know he has a reputation. You know, for the girls. The secretaries. And I thought you and him might have, too. I mean, you're so –'

'No. No. We haven't,' interrupts Kate, missing whatever he was about to say. 'Like I said, I don't even know him. And I didn't even know about the reputation. I don't really hear much gossip. I'm not really in the loop, I suppose.'

'Oh, right,' he says, grinning suddenly. 'I see. Bit of a shock, then. Sorry.'

She grins back. 'It's OK. Most interesting thing that's happened here in ages. But, I mean, I know it's none of my business, but I can't help wondering . . . if he's not gay, and you're not, how come . . .?'

'I know. Weird, isn't it. He's just . . .' Here he looks slightly wistful. 'Adam's just one of those people, I suppose. He likes sex, and he's not fussy. Broad-minded, I suppose. I know he's done it before. I hadn't, though. We'd chatted a few times, but then it just seemed to happen, really.'

Kate finds this hard to believe; how can something like that 'just happen'? But it's clear he's not going to go into any more detail without her asking some quite pointed questions, so she leaves it at that. 'I'm Kate, by the way,' she says, feeling an introduction is long overdue.

'I know,' he replies. 'Adam told me. The other night: it's not the first time he's noticed you, you know. And it's not the first time he's talked about you, either. I'm Chris.' He offers his hand, a little awkwardly. 'I've got a feeling you may be next on his list.'

It was ridiculous, but Kate had to see him. In that second, everything else was driven from her mind – including the shift she was supposed to be starting. Chris had watched her as she turned, just like that, and walked away, down the long, featureless corridor, to the lift bank.

And now here she is in the mirrored lift, twisting her hair into a hasty ponytail in the dark mirror, heart hammering, wondering what the fuck she is about to do. Operating, it feels like, under someone else's volition.

She knows he'll still be in his office; there is a pattern, a logic, to what is happening that renders her helpless, and which she knows will not end in an empty room. She knows where it will end, and her whole body is alive with that knowledge.

'Come in,' she hears from the other side of the heavy door. Why did she knock at all? Usually she just walks into the various offices and meeting rooms, assumes their incumbents have left for the night, works around them if they haven't. Now she takes a second to gather herself: she fills her lungs, exhales, straightens her spine, raises her chin. Then pushes down the stiff door handle and walks in.

Adam is regarding her calmly from behind the expensive monolith of his desk, leaning back in his chair, a pen in his hand. Behind him stretches the panorama afforded by the 90° windows of his corner office; it's dusk, and lights are coming on all over the city, reflected in the broad sweep of the river. Kate's eye picks out the winding shape of a commuter train making its way across the bridge, nosing its silent way east, leaving the two of them suspended, far above the city streets.

She looks back at Adam, and there it is: that spark again, jumping between them. She leans back on the door, making sure it's pushed to behind her. And waits to see how he will begin this.

It feels like an age until he gets up. Unhurriedly, never taking his eyes from hers, he shucks off his jacket and hangs it carefully on the back of his chair. Loosening his tie, unbuttoning the top button of his shirt, he approaches Kate across the silent expanse of carpet. When he's still a couple of feet away, he stops and regards Kate in absolute and minute detail: searching her face, examining her breasts where they push against the fabric of her top, scrutinising her hips, the shape of her, staring intently at her legs. It's both anonymous and deeply personal, and Kate submits to his scrutiny, though she aches for him to touch her.

When he does, it's a glancing touch, but one that makes her whole body shudder. He reaches out a hand as if to signal her to stop, but gently brushes her nipple with his open palm. It hardens instantly and appreciably, and she closes her eyes, feeling that irresistible confluence between her breasts and her clit, causing her pussy to come immediately to life. She keeps her eyes closed as he pinches her other nipple through the thin cloth between his thumb and forefinger, rolling it gently. She longs to step forwards and kiss him, press herself against him, but something keeps her standing there, her arms by her sides and her back against the door.

When she opens her eyes he has his cock in his hand, emerging through the opening in his trousers. He's so hard that the skin of the head is shiny and taut; she can see a few drops of pre-come emerging as he moves his hand gently but firmly up and down. The effect of such a private act performed at such close quarters, and by someone to whom she's not even been introduced, is electric. Instinctively she steps forwards, reaching for what he seems to be offering her. But it's not what he wants, not yet, and taking a step forwards Adam pins her back against the door with his forearm across her neck, his mouth hovering only millimetres from hers, but, though she strains forwards against his arm, he moves back fractionally, just before she can kiss him.

He is still masturbating, but right up against her now, his hand disappearing up her skirt with each stroke, the rhythm unmistakeable against her thigh. Before he can stop her, Kate raises one leg and hooks it behind him; suddenly, the head of his penis is pushing against the damp fabric of her knickers where they tautly cover her aching sex. She is begging him, in every way but verbally, to fuck her.

Now her pants are sopping and sticky with a mixture of her own juices and his pre-come where he is rubbing himself directly across her swollen clit. Still looking at him, Kate reaches down and pulls the fabric aside. Surely he won't be able to resist pushing himself inside her, especially when he sees how smooth and pink she is. And, indeed, she feels

Adam take a great, juddering breath as he breaks their gaze for the first time and looks down at the picture his cock makes at the lips of Kate's pussy, open and wet, displayed for him by her hand pulling the lace of her knickers aside.

But it seems he has much more self-control than she had bargained for. Moving his forearm from where it traps her against the door, he reaches around to the back of Kate's head and gently, but so firmly, pushes her down to her knees, guiding his cock into her mouth with one hand on the back of her head. Kate licks gently around the swollen head, tasting the salt of him, and runs her tongue around the shaft. He's incredibly hard, and she is desperate now to feel him inside her. But his hand still rests on the back of her head and she knows it isn't time yet. Instead, she slips one hand down to play with herself while she sucks his cock, taking him deep into her throat. Her knickers are still pulled aside and, as she kneels, it's easy for her to push her fingers inside herself, then pull them out, slick enough to tease the hot little nub of her clit where it pulses and glows.

Suddenly Adam's had enough. Roughly he pulls himself away from her, out of her mouth and, grasping her arm, pulls Kate to a standing position. Unceremoniously he turns her around, twisting one arm behind her back, and frog-marches her forwards to the picture window where he lifts her arms, placing her hands against the glass above her head. From here it feels to Kate like she's about to fall, forwards and downwards into the darkening city; but he's behind her, wrapping a hand in her ponytail, pulling her head back and pushing her skirt up. With Adam there, she can't fall.

She's already opened her legs in readiness. But what comes first isn't his cock, but his fingers, trailing a surprisingly slow progress up her thigh, over her exposed buttocks, and finally sliding into the wetness between. She feels his thumb slip into her ass, giving her an involuntary start, before his fingers begin to tickle at her clit. She is helpless now, her hands pressed on the glass, her head pulled back, her back arched, her whole body alive to what this man is doing to her.

Then, just when she thinks she can take no more, Adam's fingers are at her mouth, where she tastes herself. He lets go of her ponytail and grips her hips instead; Kate moves back a little from the glass, spreads her legs slightly wider, moves her hands down the panes so that she is steady, and cocks her ass back towards him, inviting him in.

And finally, finally, he pushes his cock deep into her swollen cunt, making her almost weep with the joy of it, the sheer shape and size of him filling her and making her close her eyes. After a few long, slow, hard strokes his hand reaches around to her clit; it seems as if all he does is pass his fingers across it and she is overtaken by her orgasm, perfectly in time with him and at his command, his hot come blossoming deep inside her, her pussy tightening around him, the two of them leaning against the cool glass.

But it isn't over yet. As she opens her eyes the first thing Kate sees is the reflection in the darkened window, of Chris, his overalls undone to the waist, his erection standing proud, his back against the door. As Adam withdraws from her, she turns and looks at the two men, a pulse starting up again somewhere deep inside, and she wonders what will become of her, working a little late tonight.

Perks of the Job Jan Bolton

What will this one sound like? Will it play an incongruously jolly refrain and set the pet dog off? Will it be the sober Westminster chime or the perfunctory shrill bell? And what will be in the porch? Wellingtons, umbrellas, old newspapers, child's tricycle, recycling boxes, broken tools? What will this garden display – attractive grasses, shingle and shrubs, a magnolia tree? And who will open the door? A busy mum, a petulant teenager, a suspicious pensioner or a self-employed, self-made tradesman? These are the factors I try to predict to keep the boredom at bay, as I conduct my door-to-door survey for the local council.

There's a familiarity to these suburban façades that's comforting, though, as if behind each door lies a sanctuary of reason and calm. It's an area of neat little enclaves where middle-class people who have chosen to eschew living at the heart of the urban sprawl can batten down the hatches and listen to *Gardeners' World* in peace. A zone of relative tranquillity that's proud to be nothing out of the ordinary.

I've been offered a lot of tea on this survey, and I've drunk it too, necessitating polite requests to use suburban bathrooms. I do love getting a nose at the décor. There have been pink shag-pile carpets and perfumed toilet roll cosies; the Body Shop shampoo collections of all-female households and IKEA flat-pack favourites for couples. I have seen tiny pale-blue opaque glass handbasins in the apartments of wealthy singles and child-friendly plastic sea creatures arranged around the bathtubs of family homes. There have been upscale designer wall cabinets into which I've stretched a guilty hand to help myself to Clarins creams – well, you have to have some perks in every job, that's what I say – and miniature perfume collections which have been cheekily dabbed at to freshen myself.

I've asked questions, collected data, handed over information packs and followed up with phone calls. All with a smile and an awareness of my training techniques in customer relations. Even though it's only a survey about energy saving in the home, I believe it is still important to look professional and not let standards slip like some of the other women on the job. I've always thought it is easier to get a better response when you look smart; it doesn't do to look shabby when cold-calling at people's houses. So, glossy hair, a business suit, make-up and some kind of heels are the order of the day. Even though this attire isn't compulsory I prefer to wear it. And I've clocked up more completed surveys than the reps who have worn trainers and sweatpants. The truth is, I actually like wearing outfits that give me authority. Flat shoes and loose-fitting tops do not make the best of my body shape, but fitted suits with jackets that nip in at the waist and pencil-line skirts slit to the knee always get me noticed. And I like that attention. I like walking along the road with a slight swing to my hips as my long hair is ruffled in the breeze. I like feeling my high heavy breasts agitated by my push-up bra, and the attention they receive from the drivers of passing cars. When I wear glossy hold-ups or stockings I always make a point of running a hand 'absent-mindedly' up and down my calves as I sit listening to male customers' experiences of their local recycling facilities – it's always such dull matters that I am obliged to research. And they always get distracted, yet they dare not say why.

And, naughty girl that I am, I like this tension. I like suburban middle-aged men. I like moistening my lips with my tongue before I answer their questions, playing with my hair and thrusting my chest at them with a coquettish giggle, especially if their wives are present. I like to tease them along to the point where they are overheating, adjusting their trousers, clearing their throats and asking me to repeat that last question, please, as for some reason their concentration wavered. I like their politeness because I know it masks a raging torrent of unrealised desires, or desires that have been trampled on by years of parenthood and conformity. It turns me on.

I don't care that much what he looks like, within reason. He can be overweight, balding, badly dressed or dull. As long as he is clean and presentable and of sound mind he is fair game for my flirtatious sport. And I've been having myself a considerable amount of fun teasing other women's husbands on this job. It can really brighten up the day if I know I can drive some guy to an erotic frenzy – or as frenzied as it gets in Metroland.

The job is actually coming to an end soon. It's lasted three months, and soon the statisticians will take over and I'll be on to my next freelance public-relations contract. Which may be just as well, as last week my little games got out of hand and it's crossed my mind there might be repercussions if my employers at the local authority ever found out. I think things are OK, but one can never be sure.

It was about 3.30 in the afternoon and I'd only been able to find a couple of houses in my designated block for that day with anyone at home. It can be the dead time for door-to-door surveys, as most people are at work or shopping between the rush hours. Anyway, I knew someone was at this semi-detached 1930s property as a Mozart piano sonata was resounding out of the open window and it did sound so very civilised and soothing. I sensed correctly that a slightly older person would be playing such music when a bloke of about fifty answered the door. As soon as he addressed me with a 'Can I help you?' I clocked that he was public school, maybe Oxbridge educated. His confident posture and tall trim body spoke of a disciplined life, and his dress was very formal for the middle of the afternoon: shirt and tie, pale-blue M&S V-necked jumper and conservative-looking dark-grey suit trousers.

I explained about the survey and its importance for predicting future local needs for waste management and energy consumption. I did this on his doorstep and it was only after a few agonising minutes during which he looked me up and down that I was invited into the hallway. Contrary to all the other domesticated men I had encountered there was a more dominant air about him. I felt for a few moments that I was going to be given a telling-off, which would have been ridiculous as, of course, I'd done nothing wrong but it was made known without anything being said that my presence was an inconvenience to this man. I didn't get a telling-off, but he completely ignored my survey and wasted no time in alluding to what he saw as an irregular situation.

'Do you usually enter the homes of strange men in the afternoon?' he asked. 'I thought there were laws about that sort of thing these days. Hmm?'

He raised his eyes at me and cocked his head to one side as his voice lifted to a questioning tone, which had about it a trace of mockery.

I laughed it off and instead flicked my manicured nails over the leaflets and questionnaires.

'Oh, I'm sure you're not that strange,' I countered, brandishing the information pack. 'You certainly don't look strange. In fact, you look like one of my old teachers.'

'Is that right?' he said, continuing to peer at me as if I were from some rare species of plant life. A thick lock of grey hair flopped over his face and his wry smile told me that he was finding it very amusing to put me on the spot, as if young female humans were fair game for sport. His eyes flashed with intelligence. He wasn't going to be impressed with my usual flighty act, so I knew I'd have to be every inch the concerned professional if he was going to even look at the survey.

He invited me into the bright and airy living room, which was spotlessly clean and tidy. A piano sat with its lid up and sheet music was open on the stand. A glass bowl of pebbles and a neatly stacked pile of magazines were placed on a long low table and two brown leather sofas of modern design were positioned at right angles to each other. He motioned me to take a seat and I accepted, my eyes casting around the room for some evidence of female occupation. It was difficult to tell; it was a rare man who kept such order in his house, unless of course he was gay, but I doubted he was. His slightly predatory demeanour conveyed his heterosexuality. The air around us crackled with curious electricity.

I launched into my spiel about the new council initiatives for garden waste collection and efficient uses of rainwater but he looked thoroughly bored by the whole thing. Throughout my cheery address he sat opposite, watching me intently, one elbow resting casually on the arm of the sofa and one long leg thrown up onto his left knee.

After a few minutes he sighed. 'My dear, I fail to see the point of all the effort when China is building a coal-fired power station every two days, or whatever it is.'

'Oh, but you can make a difference locally, and that contributes to a better sense of civic pride,' I returned. 'If we all made an effort to change just one of our habits, it would contribute so much, like turning your TV completely off, rather than leaving it on standby.'

'Is this what excites you? Recycling?' he said, in the most patronising voice I'd heard on the whole job. 'Because to me you look like the kind of girl who gets very excitable about all sorts of things. What we call a sensationalist.'

He hadn't moved, but he had delivered the first

probing question that would take the conversation away from the survey and into more personal territory.

I maintained the pretence of not realising his question was so loaded as I answered that I got excited about holidays and going out with my friends, but I felt my face flush and I immediately started playing nervously with my hair and giggling. I knew it was not the answer he wanted. And I began to feel uncomfortably self-aware and warm.

'So, I've got a little giggler in my front room, have I? I can just imagine you creating merry hell with that teacher of yours. You know what excites *me*?'

I knew it. I knew something inappropriate was about to be revealed.

'Let me guess . . . er, classical music?'

'Isn't that a little obvious? Try harder.'

'Your garden?'

'Yes, my garden. And something else.'

My face was burning. I was being brought to book. He'd sussed me out from the moment he answered the door – that I'm used to getting my own way where men are concerned, knowing all the right moves to get them in a state of anxiety. He was cleverly calling my bluff, and I was playing along with it. I began to find the situation extremely exciting. I'd never previously had any kind of sexual communication with an older, intelligent man. It suddenly felt naughty and wrong, being in this man's house, and I felt the atmosphere between us become drenched with erotic energy. I could already feel my sex becoming slippery and, as I looked him in the eyes, I felt a dart of pure lust shoot through my core. It settled as a dull ache that spurred me to carry on the playing, taking the game towards some kind of conclusion. But what exactly? Would I really let this man, who was old enough to be my father, touch me?

'Something to do with ... girls?' I suggested.

'How very delicately put. Yes, something very much to do with girls, especially girls like you.'

'What like me?'

'Spoilt pretty girls who drive men crazy and get away with murder.'

I affected an expression of fake shock and gasped to make some defensive retort but I couldn't muster the words. Instead I sat there with my mouth open, not knowing how I was going to claw the interaction back to a professional level.

'I think girls like that should go over my knee and have their knickers pulled down for a spanking. Don't you?'

Still he didn't move from his insouciant posture and that confidence made him all the more infuriating, and attractive. The salacious image he had created reverberated around my head and brought on a fresh and stronger wave of arousal which attacked me between my legs. I desperately wanted to touch myself, yet could I really let him know how he was making me feel? Supposing I'd misunderstood and this man was really just having a little joke. Or worse, that he was some kind of a lunatic and I was playing with fire. I logically concluded that an educated man with a passion for Mozart would not be the most likely profile for a psychotic and stayed exactly where I was, fiddling with my hands, my eyes darting around the room.

No one had ever mentioned spanking to me

before, yet the thought of it was all at once wildly inspiring, enough to make me giddy. It was a eureka moment; a light of realisation was turned on at that thought and, right then, I registered that there was nothing I'd rather experience than to be brought across that man's knees and dealt with – whatever that would entail.

Before I could gather the words that would form a passably coherent sentence he fired another question at me, drawing me ever closer to the moment of shame and reckoning which I so urgently craved.

'Do you think you are a girl like that? A pert little know-it-all who likes to get her way all the time?'

It would be foolish to deny this glaring truth but I knew I had to protest my character, even if I made some exaggeration for effect. It was so very very different from the kind of flirting I had experienced with men of my own age or only slightly older. Yet I felt curiously safe in his company, as if I could confess everything to him and unburden my most private thoughts yet suffer no real judgement. I intuited that I could play 'let's pretend' with him – an adult game infused with a sense of childish glee.

'I'm a girl who is usually right and my way is *always* the best way,' I proclaimed with a theatrical air of superiority.

He got up then and came to stand before me. I froze, wondering what was going to happen. Then, looking me straight in the eye, he took the pamphlets and dropped them onto the glass-topped table so they landed with a slap.

Was this it? Was he going to flip me over onto one of the sofas, push my skirt up and pull down my pants? Was he going to hurt me?

'OK, I'll think about it,' he said casually. 'Come back tomorrow about the same time. I might be in. I might not. If I'm in, I'll let you know if I can be bothered to fill in your little survey.'

My stomach became an empty chasm then. I was mortified to be strung along and then have my playful retort cruelly cut off in mid-air, just as I was beginning to understand the rules. I must have got it all wrong.

'Yes. Yes, of course, sorry, I, er . . . about the same time, you say?'

'About the same time, yes.'

It was if I had imagined the whole thing. I had never known such a sense of disappointment and rejection as being ushered out of that man's house, ashamed of my cheeky attitude, my little playing around. As I walked away, towards where my car was parked, I considered that I'd had one of those strange episodes where people drift off into trances and all sorts of bizarre subconscious thoughts float to the surface. But no, he had definitely started the conversation along a flirtatious route. And as I lay in my bed that night unable to relax, was I still experiencing the thrill of hearing him talk about spanking. I knew my intuition was correct. He *was* into it. So why did he not take things any further?

I didn't go to any more houses after his that day but – and this felt really odd, as if I had suddenly turned into some kind of a pervert – I went straight home and looked at spanking sites on the internet. Some pictures showed girls' bottoms glowing red and I wondered how much it hurt. They were dressed in kilts and white knee-high socks or old-fashioned schoolgirl outfits, while other sites that were more downmarket just had girls with their jeans pulled down.

There were women in stockings and flimsy panties being spanked by other women dressed as nurses, strict schoolmistresses and in uniforms. The majority of the photos showed girls being dealt with by older men, though, and it was these pictures that, against my better judgement and beliefs, began to arouse me sexually.

I wanted to go over the knees of some stern patriarch and feel the full force of his attention. Most prominent of the curious psychological aspects of this new-found interest was the feeling that I knew it would turn the man on as much as me. He would pretend to be all cross; and I could hide my arousal behind shouting out in heat and pain, but if and when it happened to me, I knew that I would instantly get so wet. I knew I would have to masturbate or have the man do it for me. Hopefully he would want to do it to me really slowly. It could be a kind of reward. Surely the man – whoever he would be – would be hard in his trousers and ready to fuck me. Wouldn't he? Is that what it would all be about?

I was confused, yet in an exciting way. I so, so wanted the classical music man to act on his flirtatious chat. But if he was just joking, and not really into spanking at all, then I couldn't very well ask him! He could report me to the council, and then what kind of a reputation would I get? I bit my hand when I realised my dilemma. Yet I was so turned on after a couple of hours of looking at websites devoted to erotic punishment, that I slid shamefully into my bed and abused myself in a frenzy, until I came with a violence which propelled me into a new maturity of sexual desire. I had always played the little girl act to no real end but teasing men and feeling smug about being desirable. Now I saw my charms could be used to some other effect; that I could know the pleasure of real adult games, where teasing could lead to sexual chat, could lead to spanking, could lead to . . .

The next day I took even more care about my appearance, although I couldn't be bothered any more with stringing along the usual suburban househusbands that I encountered. It was strange, but I felt I'd moved up a level from ordinary girlish teasing. I wanted something on a more intellectual level. So, instead, I affected a breezy professional tone, whizzing through about ten households and completing as many surveys in record time. I was saving all my creative energy for when I would, once again, present myself on the doorstep of my kinky stranger.

As four o' clock approached I sat in my car, checking my hair and make-up, feeling all the anticipation of first-date nerves. It was ridiculous. I was going to collect a survey from a man in his fifties who was as boring-looking as one of my dad's friends. There was absolutely no need to be fussing so much about my appearance, but still I had dressed for ease of access to my . . . oh God, to my bottom, my sex, anywhere else he might want to touch me! I was wearing a wraparound dress in pale blue, which would fall to the floor with the pull of the waist-tie. I had on shiny tan hold-ups, pale-brown peep-toe shoes with enough of a heel to give a sway to my walk and very pretty white knickers with a cherub pattern on them and satin bows at either side. I released my glossy long straight blonde hair from its ponytail and was ready, all bar a slick of transparent lip gloss.

'So, the lady from the council has come back,' was his opening line to me as I stood on the doorstep once more. The cheek! It made me sound terribly dull and old, so I immediately found myself on the defensive.

'I don't work for the council!' I blurted back. 'Gosh, that's far too boring. I'm actually freelancing for a while to get some experience of public relations.' I realised as soon as I was speaking that he was being ironic. Irony is so apt to desert me when I'm anxious or self-conscious.

'Very public indeed, I'd say. Don't you want a nice office of your own?'

'Oh, one day,' I said, flicking my hand in the air to show a spirited devil-may-care attitude, but he was right – I would like my own office for a while. 'I'm planning to go travelling for six months, so I don't want anything too permanent at the moment.'

'You youngsters,' he said. 'You think nothing of flitting off to Australia, South America. You don't know how lucky you are. That would have cost a fortune when I was your age.'

'Well, it may well cost a fortune again, once they put tax on air fuel. It will happen, you know. But anyway, talking of environmental matters, what about the survey? Have you made a decision?'

He stood aside and opened the street door wide

to welcome me inside his house once more. Again, we went through into his living room where I could see the neatly filled-out survey sitting on top of the pile of magazines. He picked it up.

'I've done this for you, then,' he said. 'I took a break from music practice and found I'd finished the bloody thing before I knew it. Didn't take long at all. In fact, it's quite interesting. I might even consider having a wormery in the garden.'

'Oh good. You've changed your attitude from the other day I see. But I do appreciate you taking the time –'

I was stopped in my flow by the magazine uppermost on the pile he had revealed. Facing me was something I'd not seen before: a glossy publication devoted to, of course, spanking. His eyes had locked on to mine; he was watching my every move: the nervous moistening of my lips, my increasing respiration rate, my dilated pupils. He took a step closer to me.

'Oh look, I've forgotten to clear away my more private magazines. Does that bother you? You look a little flustered.'

I'd not wanted to, but I immediately went into a flush of embarrassment. I brushed at my hair, put my hand to my mouth, looked at him and I honestly didn't know what to do with myself.

'Yes, I guess I am a little flustered. I've not seen any magazines like that before.'

'That's not surprising. But I must tell you that lots of women are turned on by the subject. Do you think you might be like that?'

Oh, gosh. He was forcing me to admit my new-found shame. I would have to find gargantuan amounts of courage to confess my interest but, as much as I wanted to, I couldn't bring myself to say the words.

'I, er, well, it's certainly different!' I managed, cheerily.

'That's not what I asked you, sweetheart. Shall we try again? I can see you're a little nervous. I do like it when young women get all shy. Why don't you come and sit down next to me on the sofa? We can look at some pictures together. You can whisper to me quietly what you would like.'

I went over to sit down, glad to have something to do, albeit for a few seconds. It dawned on me how useful it was to be given orders. I instantly liked that. I was meek, complicit. I felt I would do anything for him. I was, again, already wet underneath those cherubic panties.

I made myself as comfortable as I could with my arousal levels going off the dial as this tall man with his professorial air plonked himself down next to me, so matter of fact. So close our legs were touching. He could feel me trembling. His large hand went onto my knee and I felt his fingers start to circle the inside of my lower thigh. He then put the magazine in my lap and told me to look through the pages, to tell him which pictures I liked best.

It seemed like an hour passed as I flicked through those pages, so self-conscious was I of him waiting for me to speak. There was one spread that appealed to me: an air hostess in a uniform similar to my dress was being roughed up in the cockpit by the pilot. It wasn't particularly well photographed, but the combination of his uniform and her creamy buttocks, poised for his hand, set me aflame. I managed to croak out a small confession: 'I, er, quite like this one, actually,' I said.

'Like uniforms, eh? You girls are so predictable. But no more so than us men. The female form is such a distraction to us. Is that something you would like? To be spanked by an older man?'

I nodded my head. I couldn't speak. I could barely accept the situation I found myself in, in this stranger's house.

'You are very quiet compared to your first visit. Cat got your tongue?'

'No. It's just that I . . . I'd never thought about this stuff before. But I can see you're quite an expert. I don't know anything.'

'My dear, you don't need to. And I think I'd call myself an enthusiast, rather than an expert. But I can't spank you if you sit there all perfect and well behaved, can I? Surely there's something you want to tell me.'

He was right. By being silent I was doing nothing to excite him. The energy had to work both ways. It was time for a confession. So I found the courage to tell him what I'd done the previous day. About looking on the internet, getting aroused and masturbating. It was all that was needed. Within moments his crotch was swollen and my breath was ragged. I'd never told anyone such things before. Not even boyfriends. It was liberating and exciting.

He flicked the folds of my dress apart to reveal my cute knickers, the heat radiating upwards, the scent of me filling our space.

'Show me. Show me how you did it, you dirty little girl.'

I couldn't speak, but it was easy to do as he asked. I slid my right hand down in there and began to make the movements I always used. That never failed me. I closed my eyes and threw my head back as he softly encouraged me, telling me how hard it was making him.

As I gained more confidence and the act didn't seem quite as forbidden as I'd imagined, he must have sensed I was getting closer as he grabbed both my wrists and suddenly hauled me to my feet.

'Oh no you don't. Not that quickly. What do you think this is, a slut's day out? You're going to find out what happens to naughty, badly behaved young ladies who think it's perfectly acceptable to visit a gentleman in the afternoon and start playing with themselves so brazenly.'

My eyes flashed wide open in indignation. 'But you told me to do it!'

Then I realised how easily he could rile me, and I started laughing.

'Come along, giggler,' he said. 'You're coming upstairs. We'll find out who's got the upper hand here.'

So, tingling with excitement, I climbed his immaculately carpeted stairs with his hand on my bottom, up to what I thought would be his bedroom. It felt so right, yet so wrong at the same time. What would happen to me? I hoped I wouldn't start yelling, or be flaky. I'd had no experience of pain on my backside before! I didn't know what to expect. But, anyway, we bypassed the bedroom and he gently pushed me into his study. It was lined with shelves of books about music theory, historical biographies and files probably containing boring papers and sheet music.

I hopped about from foot to foot, finding the cheeky intonation he had been drawn to yesterday.

'Oh dear. Looks like I'm in sir's study,' I said, flicking my hair and affecting the posture of a spoilt teenager.

'How very observant, my dear. Who said young people weren't as intelligent as they used to be? It's their attitude we have to work on – especially that of smarter-than-thou young ladies.'

'You can't do anything to me. You're just jealous.'

'Let's see about that, shall we? You just turn around and face the window and do as you're told. I've warned you about your behaviour before, but you wouldn't listen, would you? You couldn't help yourself, you depraved little slut.'

'What?' I blurted out, feeling the genuine emotions of indignity but quickly realising the role-play aspect to the discourse. For now I would enjoy being that slut. I found my measure and joined in the game. I rammed my fingers once more into my panties and began blatantly masturbating for him. I even soaked my fingers with my juice and then rammed them under his nose. It was the final straw. Suddenly I was spun around, a hand firmly grasped the back of my neck and I was over the desk in a flash.

I felt an assured hand on my rear. If I had been shocked I would have flinched and leapt aside, but it came as no surprise. It came as a longed-for gesture of approval, for the sexual spell I had cast over him, over all of those poor frustrated suburban men. Out of all of them, it was only he who had taken the liberty; only he who was brave enough;

only he who was in a position to do so. And I was going to get it.

'That's right, don't move,' he whispered into my ear. 'Just stay calm and quiet.'

His hands began to roam all over my arse, my legs. I could feel his hard-on grazing against me as he moved about behind me. He was speaking obscenities quietly into my ear, his lascivious expression sounding all the more potent for its understatedness.

'You dirty little girls are all the same. Little cock-teasers dying for a superior man to put his hands on you.'

I went to turn around but he held me fast and gently coaxed me to lean forwards.

'You're going to stay right there, that's it, right up against the desk while I take my time with you. You are a silly girl, asking me all those boring questions in your survey about what I do with my old newspapers?' He laughed. 'I've a good mind to whack your backside with an old copy of the *Spectator*!'

I hadn't a clue what that was – some boring older man's periodical, I suppose. I was aching for the treatment he was about to dish out but, of course, I made some protest. 'No! You wouldn't dare,' I countered. 'You wouldn't do that to a council official.'

'I'd especially like to do that to a council official, but I'm not going to waste time. I'm going to give it to you the old-fashioned way – my hand on your backside, you dirty girl.'

And with that he stole a hand under my skirt and agonisingly slowly pulled down my cherubic knickers. Up came the dress, right up over my waist and neatly flattened over my back, to reveal my bare bottom and stocking-clad legs. It was time.

And then the blows came, tingling at first, then in rapid succession so hard it took my breath out of me. I squeaked and squalled but the protests were all in vain. My backside was warming up like a radiator.

'That's what you get for being cheeky to your elders and betters,' he said. 'And if you think that's all you're getting, you're in for a surprise. Stay right there, facing the window. Don't move.'

I did as I was told, but I was laughing uncontrollably. The spanking seemed to have unlocked some new gleeful part of me. I felt him busying about behind me, and then a blindfold was tied around my head.

'I don't need this,' I protested. 'I want to see.'

'It's to heighten your sensation. Remember, you are in the hands of an expert.'

I acquiesced. In one way, it actually made me feel even more liberated. He'd put on some concerto or other. It was the first time I'd had my knickers taken off to a classical score. Then I felt his hand on the small of my back and the sense that something else was about to happen. Then it landed. Like molten fire on the cheeks of my arse. I yelled.

'This is the strop – a nice thick band of leather, especially suited to the meaty buttocks of well-built girls. I could beat a symphony out of you, but you'll be pleased to know this room is sound-proofed.'

I groaned and cried out and shouted my protest as the hot lashes rained down on my poor virgin arse. It was too much. I was feeling weaker by the minute, all my spirited playfulness being literally beaten out of me. Yet, with this curious weakening feeling came a flush of something else – it must have been the endorphin rush I'd read about on the spanking websites. The heat of my flesh spread around my middle and then further inflamed my sex. I was literally desperate to be touched. It was torture to not have the attention where I needed it most. And he must have wanted to touch me, surely.

At last he put the strop aside and finally, finally, I was rewarded with the sensation of his musician's fingers against my cunt.

'It's what I've dreamt of too,' he said. 'You do know you are in the hands of a very skilled enthusiast, don't you?'

'Yes. But please, please, make me come. Please do it to me,' I begged.

'I'm teaching you patience, my dear,' he said. 'Something you have been missing, I'll bet.'

He was right. I'd been so used to getting my own way for so many years. Being pretty and blonde made life so much easier. Now I was being taught a lesson in humility, as I was begging a man old enough to be my father to bring me off with his hand. Oh, the shame!

But he worked me so skilfully. My nails raked along the sides of the desk. I began grinding my hips into the wood, uncaring that I was chafing myself, that I was displaying everything to him.

His cock rubbed against my legs and I visualised it from the confines of my blindfold. I yearned to touch his velvet hardness. I yearned to have it inside me. All I could do was groan. My stomach ached with the prolonged arousal I'd suffered – yes, suffered – at this man's behest.

He was truly skilled. He knew exactly when I was about to come because he made me ask him if I could.

'Please, sir, please may I have my orgasm now?'

It was as much as I could do to hold back those few more seconds. And then, when it hit me, it was so powerful, so extreme that I saw stars. Fireworks went off behind my eyes and I flew to the outer reaches of my universe, crying out my beautiful dirty ecstasy. And, while I was enjoying the waves that juiced my sex even more, I felt the enormity of him. He had finally entered me.

The thrusts came deep and slow. He was huge! I flopped over the desk, wanting to relax completely after my body-wracking orgasm. Surely he wouldn't take long. I couldn't believe he was that hard, that big. I laughed uncontrollably, with a sense of fun, disbelief and good humour. His hands gripped onto my sides and he pounded for a few exquisite minutes until he stopped, withdrew and leant up against my ear to say, 'I think we'll have you on the floor now.'

Still blindfolded I sank to my knees, grateful to have a new position to stretch my back and arms. Once more he pushed that amazing cock into me and I settled into the rhythm of it, egging him on with praise and thanks and dirty encouragement, completely happy now in my role as a dirty girl. Except I wasn't play-acting; I was wholeheartedly engaged in the activity.

But I slowly became aware of something near my face. Something musky and familiar – the movement of a man masturbating.

'Oh God, you dirty little girl, you know what you're going to make me do, don't you?'

It was his voice, but it was coming from in front of me. In my woozy state from the intensity of my orgasm I was disoriented. And then, before I could work out what was going on, the blindfold was whipped from my head and my friendly stranger was in front of me, pumping his huge cock in the final strokes.

'Oh yes, yes, you're going to get it all over you, sweetheart,' he said. And as a fountain of come erupted from his cock I swivelled my head around to see exactly what or who was still filling me so handsomely from behind.

She was beautiful. Mid forties, blonde hair falling around her shoulders, a strap-on harness around her hips. She said nothing but smiled sweetly and stroked my back.

I flung my head back to him as he was just coming out of his own moment of ultimate pleasure.

'Sorry, darling,' he said, somewhat breathless. 'I didn't get the time to introduce you to the wife.'